MW00760234

SCREWBALL

(the indispensable deficit)

CANARIUM BOOKS

ANN ARBOR, MARFA, IOWA CITY

SPONSORED BY

THE HELEN ZELL WRITERS' PROGRAM
AT THE UNIVERSITY OF MICHIGAN

Anne Kawala

SCREWBALL

(the indispensable deficit)

translated by Kit Schluter

Canarium Books
Ann Arbor, Marfa, Iowa City
www.canarium.org

The editors gratefully acknowledge the
Helen Zell Writers' Program at the University of Michigan
for editorial assistance and generous support.

Excerpts from this translation have appeared, in earlier forms,
in *Chicago Review*, *Seedings*, and the Poetry International
Rotterdam website. Many thanks to the editors.

Thanks also to Akademie Schloss Solitude for
making this work possible with a fellowship
for the author and a grant for the translator.

AKADEMIE
SCHLOSS
SOLITUDE

Cover: Joshua Edwards
Hölderlin Elegy, #37

First Edition

Printed in the United States of America

ISBN 13: 978-0-9969827-7-1

TRANSLATOR'S NOTE

All instances of French in the translation represent the author's use of English in the original, and vice versa. The instances of other languages remain untouched.

SCREWBALL

(the indispensable deficit)

oiseau
oiseau

hase

oiseau
oiseau

hare

hare

oiseau
oiseau

UN3'PI3RR3   hase

2

5HOT5
5HOT5

TUER

sur la neige, I see a huntress-gatheress

protected by as many skins (inside-out) as an inuit
tires like a Michelin Man™
~~form formless~~

<u>slit of the eyes</u>
glasses of

wood, ghost iron, binoculars, appears

chas,JE,se along the   *sea ice*
                             road
on the lookout for tracks and noises
sur la piste de

sur la neige, a huntress-gatheress slingshots into revolt

sur la neige, I see a huntress-gatheress
sur la neige, I glean[1]
sur la neige, it's a woman, the huntress-gatheress[2]
sur la neige, I become the movements of my heart[3]

---

1 - Notebook of the huntress-gatheress, p. 107.
2 - *Ibid.*, pp. 109-110, 123-127, 129 and 141.
3 - *Ibid.*, pp. 113 and 144.

chas,JE,se along the   *ice shelf*
                                road
on the lookout for tracks and noises
sur la piste de

on the lookout for tracks and noises,
sur la piste de, enregistré par, au passage
les bruits alentours
between them, reproducing and giving birth
in die Augen und die Ohren d'une chasseuse-cueilleuse

.

sur la neige, the huntress-gatheress
& her round tools (slingshot, bow, firkin,
cortical circumvolutions like corcules)
digging, drilling, forming, formed with
every material: wood, word, *Wort, dort, fort*
fast, *Fass*, gas, glass,
sli,
chas,JE,se
*e,*le,*ments*

sur la neige, has to learn to re
learn everything: every sign, the tracks, starting from,
& leave in thinknowing the vacation to the

************* expériment ************* validfor

> *I see, I feel, I conclude, differently*
> différemment je vois, je sens, je conclude ≈

variation of the angle, of approach ╱of attack
****
hunt
****
raise
****
cultivate
****
conserve
****
heal
****
revere
****
divine
****
bury
****
give birth
****
gather
****

:   carry on

****

gather

****

cultivate

****

raise

****

give birth

****

bury

****

conserve

****

heal

****

divine

****

chasser

****

revere

***[1]

---

1 - Notebook of the huntress-gatheress, pp. 109, 114-117, 122-128 et 142-143.

sur la neige, it's a huntress-gatheress
hunting along the   *road*
                              sea ice
white sea ice turned   *muddy floe-road*, world
in a rut, at the north pole   *piercing* the meters of millenary
ice, holes   **black**, plunging directly
      into the Arctic   Ocean

between,

paleo   .:.   mo   der   n
        some so the m e modalities have changed
                              barely
                              barrenness is
the absence from now on of great hordes like   *barren plains*
                                        paumes

sur la neige, it's a huntress-gatheress
going quickly from the green ^{QAANAAQ} country to the empire
                        to the middle kingdom^{XING}-_{PING}
        quickly
                at breakneck speed, looking for whom to hunt
                                        what
                                        to gather
                                        ▯
      upheaval of every   point of reference
north-south, east-west, no longer indicate temperatures nor
rainfall, nor winds, colds, very very cold, nor
hot, very very, it's melting where we didn't think it would and
ice where fields once lay outstretched, it's raining and
it's flooding, everything's becoming continental, marshy, and
desertlike, whatever the desert may be: sand, water, snow,
malaria and cholera, the waves have changed size

together again with *son amour.*
qui va aussi vers

steppe
après
stεp   *comme*   **tarsus**
etap   *tak*
exchange
ayes
surfaces   foot
by foot   in the face and
step by step.
surface,**d**

the
h,eart,henware) dé,**faill**,ence
ses affres se crachent   **then**
profondément trempées et her corsetry gut,skewer,s the heart
mouillées—attendent see,k ceramic her biscuit—dipped,
voi-s,e wet, baba,
s'embrocher skewered by
sucré sué droplets, sweating
of earth through
varnish, its
pearly surface (des escargot,s)
mullosque—marcher drying, dry, x times, lunacies, leaflets
ceuillir grazed, unfurl their fragrances
des griffes des oiseaux the twigs of which in one hand held,**)**
cuit des biscuits

&
1
Herzland
Oberfläsche
&

19

Sur la neige, it's a huntress-gatheress who, at the wheel of white hummer™, crosses what's left of the sea ice. Looking out for the passes, plants and animals to flee and eat, she is looking to strike twice with one stone, to survive two dangers twice. On the dashboard are mounted a P38, a knife and a switchblade, a GPS that isn't on. Riding shotgun is a buckled-in bassinet, a calm baby blows spit bubbles. Hidden under the roadmap laid out between the driver's seat and the dashboard there is, in the sunlight, a kalashnikov, a first-aid kit, and in the glove compartment, two loaded beretta 92FS's, a BIC™ lighter, an iPad™, a compass, an astrolabe. In the backseat a child watches the landscape whizzing by, he absent-mindedly pets Dzeta, whose snout rests on his lap; on the floor are two storm lamps, a kevlar composite bow, a wooden daikyu, their quivers full (sharp, plumed, and explosive arrows), pulleys, carabiners, four 8.6mm dynamic ropes, a 10mm rope. She knows how to tie every knot: overhands, double overhands, flat knots, running knots, sliding knots, lark's heads, cat's paws, reef knots, grannies, dogshanks, fireman's chairs, fisherman's knots, sheet bend doubles, overhand loops, marlinspike hitches, collars & capstan knots and carrick bends, double fisherman knots and rolling hitches, in simple figure-eight loops or in double ganses. In a timeworn satchel are a pair of cutting pliers, a leather stitching kit, a split hinge, splicing hooks, fids, a packet containing solid and hollow needles, spools of marline twine. In the trunk are crammed pelts, a tent, a deflated lifeboat, its motor, pump, oars, a seawater distiller, skis, poles, ten jerry cans of gas, piles of dried yak droppings, distress flares, a toolbox, a jack, tubs of spelt grains, rice, chicory, tomato, parsley, corn, cabbage, string beans, peas, broad beans, garlic, crates of germinating potatoes, lemons, cardboard boxes of canned foods, five 50-kilo bags of rice, ten 20-liter containers of potable water, two containers of oil, a gas camping stove, a saucepan, three bowls, a mixer, a solar panel. She bears down. And for now everything is going just fine.

At the wheel of her white hummer^{TM}, protected by the passenger compartment, having to think about having to relearn everything. Not shooting the bow or popping off her gun, but the behavior of what she will be tracking down, and the appropriate traps. Paths she will be able to take without risk. Relearning as learning that having learned won't necessarily be of use for more than a moment. A season. A landscape. Nature. Unforeseeable. Homages. Witches and wizards. What has been left behind, what accompanies her, what is to be met again, it all -merges her. Explana,quest,ions—un circuit. Which stories for the kid, in the backseat. Which gestures. Which songs. Which babblings for the baby. In keeping with. What form love will take when the reunions take place—that,   .

                                         Marches on

the white.
Disquieted by the hissing
          more resounding
      where the motor floods.

CONTINUER.

TOUT DROIT.

PLUS VITE.
PLUS VITE.
PLUS VITE.
PLUS VITE.
PLUS VITE.

SUR LA NIEGE,

The white.

The cracking.

The sea ice
gives way.
Zig-

zags,

fissures,

chasms.

Black,

liquid,

diagonal.

Sheer.

The the huntress-gatheress accelerates toward what seems the most stable,

                                expansive

breaking   apart
                  the

                                      least.

      Muted   rattling,

                                   still
                    the sea ice

          gives way.
               Everywhere.
                      Fragments
a-   drift.

Theirs,
      wide and great.
               Enough to, without danger, for a
while at least. Conditionally.   Wide
turn.
                   Off.
Engine killed. She takes a look at the baby, rear-view mirror, at the kid,
at the dog. Relaxing. If they're not worried, and she
confuses the animals for the children while taking her shortcut, that means
everything's going just fine: no danger for the time being. To be adrift
on the sheet of sea ice is neither the most comfortable nor the
most reassuring thing, but, given her height,
there are clearly worse situations,
sighs, puts on gloves, sighs, rear-view mirror, wave, steps out.

She steps out. The car door clicks shut. Cold, wind, glacial but not so bad. She takes her binoculars, looks around her: 3km to the overtaken shore. The other side cannot be seen. More would have been better, but ice is mysterious, and not being exactly in the center can be advantageous. Poker. In order to determine its height, she will have to test drill. But that would risk provoking other fissures, the devil, a faster and more ineluctable breaking-apart. Okay. 1) Determine as precisely as possible where they were when *the incident* came about. 2) Measure the speed of the wind, and try to go determine, using the knotted rope, the speed of the drift. Goes back to the hummer™, knocks, back door, on the window, soft sound, gloved, the child lifts his head, come join me, he agrees, opens up, the dog, golden retriever, Dzeta, takes advantage of the opportunity. He shuts the car door—the heat, inside, in the front seat, the baby. The huntress-gatheress whistles for the dog so she doesn't run too far off. And speaks, always with gestures, sign language, to the child. Get equipped. Take out the lifeboat. Inflate it. Get it ready for us with all the necessaries. That he unfold the tent, set up the hides. They will have it warmed up early for the two of them. That he eat and give the child something to eat. That he wait. Before nightfall, at latest, she'll be back. He agrees. She studies the map, identifies where she understands them to be and gets ready: composite bow, quiver, P38, switchblade, knotted rope, distress flares, skis, poles, headlamp, survival biscuits, 180 proof alcohol. Blows the baby a kiss, he's sleeping, she holds the child tightly against her, whistles for Dzeta to go with her; they go into the distance without looking back. The child has already gone out and inflated the lifeboat. He goes into the hummer™ to see if the baby is all right: he's sleeping. He takes a look at the map. Judging from the X she drew on it, he thinks that perhaps her calculations were not precise. We'll see tonight, by the stars. He takes out the hides, puts them in the tent, puts the baby inside, who does not wake up. And continues to fill the lifeboat, knowing the weight of the maximum load, and adding, to that of the objects he piles in, their four bodies. He gets in, prepares something to eat, wakes the baby up and feeds it.

Changements. Un et leur. Là. La nature change.
Gris et vert grandissent. Noir et bleu se brouillent. Le jaune crie doucement.
Dedans est un devenir. Dedans se répand dans
le paysage. Le dehors change, sourd. Blan. Ven,t
rouge, blanc, violet, rose, le blanc respire, trois vies. Enter. Se déplacent comme, sont:
graine, à côté de, casse the grain husks, without madness nor in the flower rifle.
Simplement, gentil, le rituel dans les champs de pierres, où
entre deux, pas, le crâne d'un renard se tresse maintenant aux
autres, vœux, qui partageant un côté, cheek-to-chick, side, seeds,
dehors, ensemencent la mer, le lagon, the lacuna, au-dessus de
l'océan, partout, du point à la ligne—couché, longé de mousse, weak, wake, wave,
ses forces douces & violentes. Quelque chose se passe.
Existe-t-il la choix parmi. Monter une chimère chimique, ou être écrasé,
Exsuder en tout cas. Ou transpirer. Respirer. Doux & violents, étranges,
ses pas. Ses forces.

25

Sur la neige, the huntress-gatheress skis toward her white hummer™. It is still light out, the day is long, and the wind is blowing, the weather is nice, a pink, blue, purple, wide, clear sky. Speed measured, high speed of drifting, for the moment it seems consistent—how much time before the sheet starts to break apart, how much time before it touches land, ice? Dzeta frolics. Roots around. Sniffs, seems to have found a trail—aside from hummer™'s. The huntress-gatheress looks: nothing yellow, the whites, the greys, enormous. Some animals, drift, with them, trapped, here, on this raft, could be: meat. Fear, hunger and courage. Knows them knowing her reactions to; thinks up dances and chants; slippage felt, totem, she smells their hides, and, covered by them, knows that she isn't—animal, not enough. The huntress-gatheress skis toward her white hummer™, the kid and the baby. Toward eating. To study the map with the kid, to look at the stars and determine their position. Then to sleep. And then to wait. And while waiting, train him to draw from, and to draw himself out of, every situation, to teach him everything, to teach him everything that she knows. And while waiting for this time of waiting, to hum:

> *ich*
> *brauche* d'*ein* u, *ein* y, of a
> junction, I rediscover the
> multitude of paths opened by play   murmur
>   branch, *Zweig*, stone, *Stein*, Man, *Mann*, walk,
> *une érrance inquisitrice Wandern* that allows for fear, *die*
>   *Angst, la peur, die Mitleid*, pity, *tant pis, Witz, calembour,*
>   pundrum, between Pythie *und Freud*, to slaughter a cock
>   reading its hot and steaming entrails is one way of re-rolling the dice,
>   the dreams, the runes, écrasé, jeu, échecs, the cheat, *la poitrine d'*
>   *ein Schachspieler, ein Spiegel, a miroir d'un* mirror, reflection,
>   a failure, *ein Ausfall, un échec, une rose est eine Autobiographie*
>   *est tendre* buttons *et toute chose est un monde, die Welt,* the world,
>   Ida, *Ida, Ida, la magie* magic *von die Magie*, la mort, *die*
>   *Tod, das Gesetz, die Berg*, au sommet, *la montagne, la loi, la*
>   *mort*, law

From afar, it stands out and shines, too easy to see, tempting for all potential predators, what lives feeds, the half-orange of their shelter. Out of place, thus attractive, frightening, then, to attack—defense. She wonders if the kid stayed behind to keep watch from the hummer™, or if he took cover, or if he found yet another solution—in this case, one for the baby. She moves forward, approaches; from a distance that could prove dangerous for them, something is jingling. Not so bad, but it sends a warning from both sides. The wind could carry the sound too far, on the other side, so he couldn't hear it. She observes the apparatus: net like a spiderweb, the raft-tent at the center: someone is approaching, he knows it. He moves forward. Suddenly blinded, she protects her eyes, sees him aiming at her, flashlight & kalashnikov—disproportionate. She gives him the sign to drop it, thumb-index O, O!, everything is ok. Dzeta runs to join the kid. Squinting, the light still dazzling her, from a distance, gestures, no speech, to describe: the ice patch is drifting at 5 knots—more or less. She makes out its movements, backlit, it's too fast, the wind isn't strong enough, the patch is in the process of breaking off. She points to her legs: there—there, you'd feel it in your legs. You couldn't tell if it was going to break. It was a risk, you know as well as I do. Look, we've got the raft, there's nothing dramatic going on, even if we have to navigate; we'll wait for the stars. He lowers his arm, the lamp. She has returned, healthy and safe. She was just able to return: she has returned: everything is ok. He deactivates the traps, runs to join her, holds her in his arms. Under the pelts, her belly against his cheek. Ok. Once the moment is over, she gestures to him that she wants to check he hasn't forgotten anything. I'll come find you right away. Is the baby doing ok? Yes. Ok. Run. Dzeta will go with you. I'll be back soon. He goes back into the tent. She checks the hummer. Looks in the front and back, on the ground and in the map pockets. Ok. She comes back out, opens the trunk. He did good work. He's becoming ready. She opens the tent's flap. She baits the traps, closes the flap, opens the tent's door, the warmth assails her, goes in and closes back up immediately.

It's nice out, it's hot. The baby's still sleeping. She listens to him, checks his breath, regular, touches his forehead, cool. The child is sitting, wrapped in pelts. Same gestures for him, her hand, then her lips, on his forehead. He shuts his eyes, opens them again—sleep? No. Not yet. Ok, I'm going to sleep for an hour, wake me up in an hour, the stars will be out. We'll be able to find our way. Then you can sleep when it's your turn. I'll keep watch tonight. Ok. She lies down. She shuts her eyes. She falls asleep immediately. The child watches her. Déjà vu, but he's learning again; to be able to fall asleep immediately. To sleep quickly, deeply. Her breath already slows. Already her eyes are moving under their lids. She dreams. She hasn't eaten, she fell asleep, she'll eat afterward, he'll sleep afterward. Suddenly to do the most important thing. The most important thing. He doesn't want to forget. He repeats to himself: The most important thing. To do suddenly the most important thing. How does she go about choosing the most important thing? To always choose the most important thing? How doesn't she hestitate, when, suddenly, without hesitation, she is doing the most important thing? This, too, he mustn't forget to ask her. How she does it. To ask her in a bit. When she wakes up. Before he falls asleep. To ask her. So she explains. So he knows. So he learns. The baby stirs, eyes shut. He pushes gently on the basket's edge, gentle swaying, there there, gently rocking. In our legs. If it cracks, we'll feel it there, in our legs. He focuses to see if he feels anything whatsoever. Nothing. The wind outside is blowing. Blowing less than a moment ago. When did it weaken? Before or after she fell asleep? He looks at his watch. 10:36pm. He'll make note that, at 10:36pm, the wind weakened. Are they advancing less quickly now? Why didn't she look and make a note right away on the map when she came back? The map is folded up, there, at her feet. Wasn't the most important thing knowing where they were in order to know the speed at which they were drifting, and toward where? How many days can they hold up at sea if the ice patch breaks again?

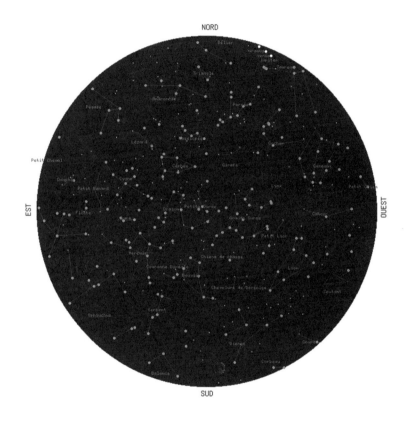

NORD

SUD

EST

OUEST

Now that we're drifting, we shouldn't be far from JAN MAYEN. But I don't know what would be better: trying to make landfall or to keep drifting. I doubt our iceberg is approaching it like that, the currents are too strong. On one side, when the patch breaks apart, if it breaks apart, it could be dangerous. But on JAN MAYEN there is no one, there is nothing to live on. And nothing on which to get off it. And leaving would be more complicated than navigating by sight toward Greenland, Iceland, or Norway. What do you think, kid? He shakes his head. He doesn't know. If he doesn't know, can she know? Instincts, you know, they don't learn themselves. That's why I'm asking if you have an idea, some hunch? He shrugs his shoulders, a sign of powerlessness. We'll wait, then, we'll figure it out. Let's rest here in the meantime. We're ready to fend off a good deal of eventualities for now. We'll wait, then. It's not the simplest thing, waiting with nothing to do. But finding rest in the fatigue of waiting is truly difficult. You have to learn that, too. To find rest in that. To keep busy, rest, keep busy. To do both just as often and with the same commitment. She grumbles and spies the horizon through binoculars, trying to discern the line of the island's mountains. No birds yet, perhaps tomorrow. Tomorrow no doubt we'll see JAN MAYEN appear on the horizon. I'm going to take care of the baby. The kid doesn't react, he didn't see her say this last phrase, busy spying the horizon. He goes back toward her, although she has already walked away. He runs to join her, passes her, and stops in front of her. I want to go see the edge of the ice patch. It's dangerous. Even if I don't think the ice patch is ready to break, I don't know a thing. What will you do if you find yourself all alone on a chunk of ice drifting who knows where? Huh? You wouldn't die from cold or hunger. You'd die from throwing yourself into the water because you'd have been so hungry and so cold, and you'd prefer a quick death. Is that what you want? He looks at her. But you, you've been there. The first day, you were there. Yes. I've been there. But you, you won't go.

He frowns. If I have to learn, I have to learn that too. That fear. You too, you should learn the fear for me. She makes an evasive hand gesture. And you know it. He points his finger against her chest. There, he adds, his lips shut, there, you should learn it there, striking, this time, the palm of his hand against her breast, and, under her breast, her heart. She turns her face away, looks into the whiteness. Seeking time, seeking in her heart, something to say to the kid, some answer to give him. He's right. She isn't afraid for him when she goes away. All right. All right, she looks at him and says ok. Ok, that's fine. Ok, go ahead. When you are ready, come find me in the tent. Come tell me when you go. She goes quiet. She doesn't move. She says to him, you should learn that pride—it's not always a good thing. It may help you stay alive but more often it will lead you to your death. She leaves him, goes back in without looking at him. The baby was awakened by her storming into the tent; the kid hears her crying. He remains standing, in the wind, the cold. Gripped by hesitation. Standing between the white hummer™ and the raft-tent, frozen with doubt. She talks to the baby, tells it that she is going to give it something to eat, change its clothes, she sings in a soft voice, so softly she tells him that everything's ok, that JAN MAYEN is close and that she doesn't know if they're going to make landfall. She hums. He imagines the baby playing with her fingers, grabbing the huntress-gatheress', grabbing her hair. The kid goes into the tent and asks her for his binoculars, I need to be able to see, don't you understand? Yes. Here you go. She holds them out to him, and already the baby begs for them. The kid looks at them. Sighs. She raises her head to him, looks at him, smiling. He goes back out, adding nothing. The kid climbs onto the hummer™'s hood, then onto its roof. Looks through binoculars at the horizon. The whiteness, and further off, to his right, the whiteness giving way to the blue-black of the ocean. He looks for JAN MAYEN and the line of its crest. He looks to the other side. No one, nothing, has arrived yet, but you never know. You never know. He should keep watch while. She lies down, the baby against her; she falls asleep,

happy,
so happy, I gush I
flood and flow and flow, I
soak the sheets and spread myself out on the
floor, indivisible and divided, I flood and flow
and flow between the planks, to the door, under the
door, I slide, I snake, I cascade, cascade, cascade, I
bound, jump, walk, walk, walk, splash from stain to
stair, I mingle with the lime and soak the wood, I cascade
and launch, I gush there over a skull, over the astrolabe,
there over the U of a half-unrolled map, I soak the paper,
the ink runs, a lake is decribed, cascades, I cascade, from
stain to stain, cascade, the wax repels me, it splits me,
droplets, immiscible I drip, I seep, I gush, I flow,
gush, explode, a lake empties out, I am a lake and
a fountain, indivisible and divided, flow, flow,
absorbed by the sheets, the blanket, the cotton, I
spread out, puddle, at the foot of the stairs,
I spread out, I shake under light
steps, hands
like a conch

Close now. the summit of JAN MAYEN mixes into the very low, spiraled, and twisting clouds. Dropping the binoculars, held up by a cord around her neck, she turns toward the tot: pretty, isn't it? He nods, he explains, pointing out the crests, his fingers roll up, the crests form these swirls. She looks again at JAN MAYEN. Against her back, sitting in the amauti, the great hood of her coat, she feels the baby stirring. She says to the tot, it will still be pretty from afar. I don't see any boats. No planes. Nothing but the sky moving over this island. Either JAN MAYEN has been evacuated. Or the people who are there don't care much for receiving guests. He nods. Their hands as visors, turned entirely toward the island, they look out. The kid's hand just rested on her arm, she turns around: he has a nervous air, asks for the binoculars. What did you see? He doesn't answer. Tense, he observes. Brusquely turns toward her. Indicates a point to look at with the binoculars. She takes them, looks, looks at the kid. What? In the air the kid's hands sketch the conical form of a volcano, JAN MAYEN is a volcano? The huntress-gatheress shakes her head, what? The tot's hands stir, clarify, to the right, the fourth peak, look. She obeys. A darker veil descends, could it be an eruption? Clouds, a nuée ardente, how to tell? A storm that breaks out just like that, is it possible? Everything is possible, she knows this, but it's a matter of knowing how to react, of knowing that everything is possible, and reacting in the best possible way. If it's a storm, the risk that it move toward them isn't insignificant, she looks at Dzeta, relaxed, at their feet—if it's a storm, the electricity hasn't thrown the dog into a panic yet. Whether storm or eruption, it means there's going to be a tempest. One hell of a tempest. The raft is ready. In the amauti, the baby stirs. She and the kid suddenly feel their legs shake, feel that the vibrations are passing into their bodies. The squall picks up, the current drags them quickly toward the island: the ice patch is going to break. The patch has held on till now, but faced with such a current, it won't hold. Get in the raft, NOW!

They climb out of the hummer™, go back into the tent. Inside, they check the straps holding everything down, tighten them. It groans. Louder and louder. The cracking of the ice screws into their eardrums. They concentrate, prepare to be thrown toward, into, the sea, to be forced to keep away, to fight, whatever's going to happen, in order not, or as little as possible, to be hurt, to be able to react as soon as the first shock hits, to react as quickly as possible. It roars. The dangers, their probabilities, flow past, assessed; considering the movements they may have to make in the coming seconds. And then nothing, a great calm. That lasts. The kid relaxes the muscles in his neck, rolls his head down, eyes shut, opens them: Dzeta looks at him, panting, smothered by his thighs. He unclenches his legs. NO! The kid jolts, immediately tenses, tugs on the rigging, refastens it. More gently, she adds: stay focused, this isn't the time to relax, it might come back any second now, you've got to be ready. The kid sees the baby—its lips are quivering, it starts to cry. The huntress-gatheress tries to cradle it, her shoulders rocking. Through clenched teeth, with difficulty, the kid murmurs. Red. She repeats: red? Lava? The cloud was coming from the volcano? You saw lava flowing before it started? All is still and ready to break, inside their shelter and out. The baby is no longer crying. There is the density of a calm—artificial. Still. Nothing happens. She repeats: stay focused. And it's going to come very slowly. Very slowly they perceive the beginning of the slope. The eruption caused a wave whose angle gradually augments. The ice patch is thrust toward JAN MAYEN. Its incline swells. Smoothly. The raft begins to slide, slowly. Too close, they hear the grinding of the hummer™. Topples, falls back, crashing, the baby screams. Topples from the side to the roof, crashing, it speeds up, they move forward and slide, the sound multiplies, drowns out the baby's screams, gnashes, topples, rolls, flips, passes them, doesn't crush them, disappears. Chaos, faster and faster, the huntress-gatheress' fear now is the frozen escarpment that could tear a hole in the bottom of their raft.

UN3'PI3RR3

7H3Y F4LL D0WN

ext. - nuit
the shocks
are too
numerous,
too vio-
lent, too
int. - nuit
repeated,
reverberat-
ed in their
arms arced
over the
rigging.
Around
them,
the half-
orange of
their raft
like a point
lost in
the swells
and the
air, frenzy,
the end of
the world,
int. - nuit
chaos,
a series
of waves
breaking
onto the
island,
Beeren

moving away, a group
castle—marriage,
birthday,   tipsy people. The group breaks up
and re- groups   walks and some conversations.

one's window

from behind, perceived
taking up
movements of gazes   to move away
watch your feet   from which
look   —and now   a man, a
woman   another man   pay for the

, they're laughing together, wishing
each other   in the building
watches the scene, while
the two   other wing. The woman
the window watches now straight
snowy panorama   low-angle shot over the forest,
dark, marking a border.   some
eyes, the other   disappeared whil

From an angle   moving toward
lamp,   in an armchair, to take a
almost immediately.
on a   packet of   a lighter. She

C'était l'année dernière.
Ai-je autant
changé, alors ?
Ou fais-tu semblant
de ne me pas reconnaître ?
Déjà un an,   ich kann verlieren, aber ich immer giwinnen
peut-être plus que ça.   *at*
Toi, au moins,   Mariánské Lázně
tu es toujours la même.   I can lose, but I always win
Tu as toujours   je peux perdre, mais je gagne toujours
a royal castle
royal like paradise, in the night, between the blinds, the lights burn
in, visi, ty   and shine in the spaces
                           laid with parquet floor and silent there
                                   .l.
                                        windows thrown open
                     speech act   the short expanse
                     can occur
                                        green or white, the forest
                                   obscure

           un trou noir   comes to take the place
           a black hole   in
           ein schwartzes Loch   the western part of the city to
           maison   1 trou
           home   , the black
        die Nacht (schöne)
           Haus,
           Gern verlass ich diese Hütte, / Meiner Liebsten
           Aufenthalt / Wandle mit verhülltem Tritte / Durch
           den ausgestorb'nen wald. / Luna bricht die Nacht der
           Eichen, / Zephyrs melden ihren Lauf, / Unde die Birken
       streu'n mit Neigen /   déneige **et**
après   tout
                                                     neigen, bend,
after all   s'incline,   T, Tender
       immerhin   *verlieren*   *immer*   **en   d**
                                              hin   tendre
                                                        l'encens le plus doux
            les mêmes yeux rêveurs ...
               le même sourire ...
             la même rire soudain ...
            le même mouvement brusque
                   du bras ...
          le même manière de poser ta main
       sur ton épaule ... et tu mets toujours le même
           parfum. Souviens-toi ... les bois ...

                         38

                    lights u   - b e r g ,
  almost   da   **s,now*,s**   where   e r u p t i n g ,
  will almost consume   **a**   in the noise   the   lava,
        of the   ***,days,*** of the laughter   the stream,
                          looks out the window   s u c c e s -
        what it means to love, in   **int. - nuit**
        question, beyond the over-ideal idea   sions   of
        how   t y p h o o n
                          point and colors   b i r t h s
                                                      ext. - jour
              crumbles, faced with fear,   in   the
                  no longer monstrous   whirlpools
                                                      of Karam,
  In the   snowy forest   skirts a   i c e b e r g s ,
        frozen lake,   bridge, and   b o u l d e r s
  distant   **int. - jour**
        land, then runs off.   torn   away,
        The boar rifled through   *sauerkraut, sauna* and houses
                          a half-buried couple   rising there
  entwined, frozen, appears   a l o n g -
    apesanteur,   side them.

    curiosity   in wood,   books
  and objects, windows, etc.) is   breaking
  of earthenware.   even though
              day   when I approach
              vase, a   it stands in for
    on the edge of   a bright face
  Against   and bright, the rest returns to shadow
  complementary. It serves them   drops off
              from up close   closes
        hands, then the eyes   leaves,
                                        of soda
          next to pieces of   , sigh
  a   to the lips, goes in: *We are not there yet.*

THE SPIRAL BATH, [1, 2]

In the southern hemisphere of our earth
there exists a fairly common species of migratory bird
They multiply so fast
that only a ruse of nature
can keep us from a nightmare
Every year their flocks darken
the skies of western Africa
where they gather to migrate
over the Atlantic
Only a tenth makes it to South American shores
ninety percent fall exhausted
into the Atlantic
One imagines that in the middle of the ocean
where according to geologists
millions of years ago
Africa broke away from the Americas
these birds begin to spin around
They search for their country
where it no longer exists
Their instinct passed down over millions of years
leads them to their deaths
Only the most insensible make it to the new continent

1 - Rebecca Horn in *Rebecca Horn*, with texts by Doris von Drathen, Sergio Edelsztein, Martin Mosebach and Rebecca Horn, Institut für Auslandsbeziehungen e.V., Stuttgart & Carré d'Art – musée d'art contemporain de Nîmes, 2000, p.76.
2 - Notebook of the huntress-gatheress, p.111-113.

THE SPIRAL BATH, [1,2]

In the southern hemisphere of our earth
there exists a fairly common species of migratory bird
They multiply so fast
that only a ruse of nature
can keep us from a nightmare
Every year their flocks darken
the skies of western Africa
where they gather to migrate
over the Atlantic
Only a tenth makes it to South American shores
ninety percent fall exhausted
into the Atlantic
One imagines that in the middle of the ocean
where according to geologists
millions of years ago
Africa broke away from the Americas
these birds begin to spin around
They search for their country
where it no longer exists
Their instinct passed down over millions of years
leads them to their deaths
Only the most insensible make it to the new continent

1 - Rebecca Horn in *Rebecca Horn*, with texts by Doris von Drathen, Sergio Edelsztein, Martin Mosebach and Rebecca Horn, Institut für Auslandsbeziehungen e.V., Stuttgart & Carré d'Art – musée d'art contemporain de Nîmes, 2000, p.76.
2 - *Notebook of the huntress-gatheress*, p.111-113.

Very far away, the silhouette of an iceberg. Now, the calm, the rolling, the chatter of birds, around and above. Certain ones fly overhead, others swim beside the craft. They observe—eyes round, sidewise. A first steamer duck climbs over the raft's tubing, quickly followed by others. A black skimmer places itself on the dome, slightly crushed, a Magellanic oystercatcher comes to fight for its place. Alternating cries, menacing gestures, opening in each movement of their wings to full span, they have it out on the canvas and start to break through it. The smell of death, shit, and piss rises. The wind picks up and drives them off, leaving the drifting, open raft to the waves and rain. Water seeps into their clothes. Frozen. Streams over their faces. Flows. Shoulders, chest, back. Rain. Waves. The raft fills up, sags, their legs half submerged, danger. Torn from, violence, a spasm, the cold wakes her. Confused, she tries to move. The rigging prevents her. She makes out the torn tent, the face of the kid, Dzeta between his legs, facing her in the half-light. They aren't moving. Nor is the baby, against the back of her neck. She tries to speak but isn't able. Drymouth. Stiff body. Reflex: if the rain, if a wave, the raft flips, I'm attached to it, I die. Stiff body. The fingers. She focuses. Black. Her index finger. Her thumb. Her index finger, her thumb, the middle finger. Her middle finger, her index finger, the thumb, the ring finger. Her middle finger, her pinky. Her index finger, her thumb, the middle finger, her pinky, her ring finger. Her hand. The other one. Her thumb, her index finger. Her hands respond. Her arms are immobilized. With her weight, she jostles the rigging too tightly wrapped around her arms. She contorts, shoulder popped out of the socket, slips again further into the freezing water, which steeps the bottom of the raft and at last she can free herself—right shoulder, arms, half her body is free. Black. A wave could sink the raft. She is still attached. It has to be finished. Numb, the huntress-gatheress opens her eyes again. Half-darkness. Shuts her eyes. Runs her hand along the rigging again. By feeling, the last knots are untied. Her hand grasps the strap, she climbs again onto the tubing where she had tied herself down, reflex, not to die drowned in the bottom of the raft.

ext. - nuit

vista over goes down valley,
Ici, autour, dans **dans les champs d'herbe, les promenades sont**
soaked, sits upon, fallen, form
motifs **au-dessus, une herbe** é, comme une **forê vert**
bridge mossy on stream
tapis **feuillage en-dessous** **décrit pas,**
is aiting for not very many ill
pas de peintre, chaque nuance de vert, vert-jaune, vert-bleu,

vert- **, vert-f** **, vert-** **et** **alors**
surprised by sounds a of animals, crushed
compose **dans ces** **coloré**
moss, listen to this chirping, When
lignes. Lire un autre motif entre
lève, out of breath, goes down the
face **le motif de la lettre volée entre le**
running e allows hill reeds
coloré and the leaves the ground
So a distance
crié, que

"T'es en retard. t'attend, là
sans cesse?
Tu sais,
gémarmeladant
plus tôt.

Même aigre
Autrement **va enfin**
te tuant.
Its height, at the bottom

doux
"J'ai perdu

lace

revient toujours très vite... non?

43

5HOT5
5HOT5

It's kicks in her legs that wake her up. It's day out—high sun, cold. In the wind, the canvas of the tent claps. Kicks in her leg. The kid. With his heels, the kid hits her to wake her up. The huntress-gatheress sees Dzeta's body, swollen with water, floating on the surface of the water contained by the raft. Her violet tongue hangs out of her mouth, her rolled up cheeks reveal her fangs and jaw, clenched. Kicking her legs, still. The fury on the kid's face. She moves, crawls, drags herself over to him and starts to untie the knots imprisoning him. The kid's hands are burning. Panic-stricken, the same fear as hers—a wave, the raft flipped over, to die now, drowned, he pulls on the ropes which, soaked, tauten. Unable to speak, unable to smack him to make him stop, she pauses her gesture. Lifts her hand, clenches her fist while looking him in the eye. He pants. Calms down. His knife. His serrated knife. Hooked to his belt, in its sheath. She checks around his waist, finds it, takes it out, cuts the straps, the kid's wrists are free, now his arms. His last strength passed into his fear, dying drowned, tied up. He falls into the huntress-gatheress' arms, his head against her neck, turns his face to the baby, whose eyes and mouth are closed. He shuts his eyes. He feels her push him away, clings to her, she sits him down, no longer holds him up, the effort of supporting him exhausts her, the raft pitches—drowned if he falls, he holds on. He opens his eyes. Sees her, from behind, open the crates. Dzeta floats, the purple of her tongue. He closes his eyes. Pitches. Opens. The huntress-gatheress is next to him, the waterproof pack, red, from the medical kit in her hands. She is feverish, tries to open it, shakes, needs antibiotics, anti-inflammatories, vitamins. Success. Needs water. She makes for the stern of the raft. From the water, emergency blankets in her hands, it pitches, comes back. She holds out the pills to the kid. He opens his hand, docile, closes it again, still. She pours some water into his mouth, he swallows, she slips the pills through his lips, she pours some water into his mouth, he swallows. When it's her turn, she, water, pills, water. Swallows.

45

Looks at him, his face, eyes shut, lips blue, shivering, wrapped tight in the fur amauti, soaked, takes his gloves off, the kid's hands, swollen, covered in frostbite. She holds back from rubbing him to warm him up, tries to take off his anorak, sleeves, pulls, no, standing above to pull it off him, down-up, it pitches, the tot's arms in the air, impossible, it's pitching too much, she sits and, with a knife, cuts in. Puts the strips down beside them. Underneath, the bright zippers slide open. Undresses him. Sweatshirts. T-shirt. In piles. His torso, naked, pale, weak. Takes out an emergency blanket, covers his shoulders with it. She shakes, her fingers are numb. He hasn't moved, eyes shut, lips blue. He fights, motionless, to hold himself up— sitting. She folds his arms, places his hands in his armpits and presses his elbows against his body. With your legs now, hold on with your legs. His thighs contract. Hold on. She brings her face close to his, touches his forehead with her lips. Too hot. Looks at his, her hands on his cheeks. He fights. I'll be back. Keep holding on. Slowly, clinging to the raft's rigging, swaying, weighed down in her own soaked clothes, she makes for the stern of the raft. To save him. Her gestures are slow, within them all the energy she has. To save them. Each of her gestures is held out toward—saving them. Now. To save them, now. Now. Potable water, cans of potable water—enough? Now. Yes. Now. After, if after, the distiller. She finds the dried meat, too soaked to be edible. She looks at Dzeta. Have to throw her overboard. Before she starts to rot. After. First find something to eat. A box, a box of anything. There. She goes back to him, arms full, balance dizzied, trudges through the water in the raft. Sits down, makes him drink, finishes the can—finished, slides, and floats. Dzeta. Something to eat now. She opens a box—the kid doesn't react, he holds on—on the edge, he holds on. She moves toward him, plunges her fingers into the box, takes out some bits of meat, puts them into his mouth. He is unable to chew.

She feeds him, after chewing for him, sliding the paste from her mouth into his. After half the box, she begins to eat. Feels her body relax. To sleep. Not to sleep now, to keep on, to try to save them, to go on. Looks at the kid. Who is sinking, won't be able to keep sitting up. Rub him. Movements. Hers, to keep him sitting up—on the threshold. Back of the boat, finds oil, comes back, her hands under the golden blanket, back, stomach, shoulders. Hold on. Again. Keep holding on, it's going to be ok. Imperceptible nod of the child's head. I'll be back. Undresses herself. Tries not to take off her fur anorak, takes the knife, repeats the gestures, cuts in, knife against her chest, the vivacity of the cold against her naked skin. Cautiously removes the anorak, one arm, slides from her back to her shoulder the weight of the baby in the amauti. The other arm, takes the amauti in her arms, kisses the baby's face. Now. Cuts off the amauti. Goes back to the tot, opens the edges of the emergency blanket, places the amauti on his knees, coats the baby's face in oil, closes the golden blanket. Hold on. Ok? She goes away again, takes off her other clothes. Piles them up. Lighter by gallons of water. Naked, her skin, the wind, the cold. Reinvigorates. Rubs herself with oil, thin protection, but protection. Waves. Dzeta drifts toward her. She would rather the kid be awake. Having to put the dog in the water without him makes her uncomfortable. Later. First bail out water, put the tot to sleep, give him more antibiotics, anti-inflammatories, repair the canvas, lay out their clothes. Then wrap herself up in an emergency blanket, eat again, let herself go to sleep. Afterward get up again in the night to look at the stars, try to understand where it is they find themselves. After. Dzeta knocks against her leg. It has to be done. She drags her to the edge of the raft, where the tent is torn and pushes her into the water. The body slides in and continues to float. Soon devoured by fish. She hopes nothing bigger, more dangerous, will be attracted by the corpse. Murmurs. Shuts her eyes. She turns back. Bails out water. She unties the knots holding down the waxed canvas, cuts, hooks them into eyelets, carabiners, adjusts the height of the rope. Canvas bucket. Bails out water, slowly. Teeth clenched, body in pain. This weakness. Provokes anger. Calms down. May this rage pass as she dries the boat. Is exhausted. From time to time, she looks at the kid. Sitting, straight up, maybe asleep. Now, keep bailing out water. Bails. Bails. Bails. Bails. Bails. Bails. Bails. Bails. Bails. Bails. Bails. Bails. The kid, maybe asleep. Bails. Bails. Bails. Bails. Bails. Bails. Bails. Bails. Bails. Bails. Bails. Bails. Bails. Bails. Bails. Sitting, straight up, motionless. Bails. Bails. Bails. Bails. Bails. Bails. Bails. Bails. Bails. Bails. The kid, asleep. Asleep. Spreads another emergency blanket on the bottom of the raft. Takes the amauti, in one arm. Wakes the kid up, makes him lie down on the blanket. Lying down. On his belly, sets down the amauti, crosses his arms over, she puts the tot's arms back in his armpits. Takes off his pants and tights. Rubs his arms, greases them with oil. The survival blanket spread back over them, the baby and the kid, his face now edged with gold. Give him something else to drink, antibiotics, anti-inflammatories, vitamins. She opens another can, lifts his head, puts a finger between his lips, pours water in, slips the pills onto his tongue, makes him drink again, closes his mouth back up, he gulps with difficulty but swallows, she places his head back on the bottom of the raft. She drinks. Now, before, now, remounts their shelter—as much as possible. The rings, stick them in their eyelets. Extend the canvas from them, even if torn. Stitch them back up, yes. It's necessary, later, now tend to the most urgent. To make shelter. Makeshift shelter but, should hold up for a night, keep out rain, waves. She spreads out the furs, the clothes, that they dry—a bit. Looks, finds another box, eats, squatting at the stern, back against the crates, she chews slowly, watching the kid sleep under the canvas awning. Now to close the shelter back up. And then sleep.

Searches ahead, finds a flashlight, tests it, it works, leaves it on, resting against the crates. Ok. Close the awning. Pulls the canvas from the middle of the raft to the stern, crouching, hooks it over the crates, folded, too low to keep standing, asymmetric shelter—shelter. In the half-light, and the lamp's beam, she **what separates,** takes it and, crawling, joins the tot. Turns it off **the distance** before slipping under the emergency blanket, **by which humans** placing herself next to him. His sleeping body **are separated** is burning up. She removes the amauti from the tot's folded arms, his hands still jammed in his armpits, holds the baby against her breast. It must have been three days, three days at most, unconscious three days at the most, otherwise they would all be dead. When she opens her eyes, she feels the tot staring at her, she and the baby in her arms. Through the canvas's hemstitch, where she didn't fix it to the raft, filters a red glow—dusk? Dawn? Grows used to little light, the huntress-gatheress now makes out the kid, on his forehead beads of sweat. The amauti in one arm, with the other moving the covers aside. She places the amauti gently on the bottom of the raft, kneels over the boy. With her hand, she wipes his forehead. He needs medicine again. Feels blindly, finds the lamp. Sweeps the space. Ok. First some water. Stern. Comes back. Medical kit. Ok. Hands him the can. Still too weak. Makes him drink. Takes the pills, mouth, water, he swallows. Better— even so. Takes the kid's hands in hers, looks at them—gently. The frostbite left traces—nothing irremediable. She applies the oil again, hand-to-feet, rubs him down, neck, shoulders, chest, belly, groin, sex, thighs, calves, ankles, feet, toes. Arms, hands. The kid looks at her, looks at the baby, looks at her again, she has turned her eyes away, stood up. Feels her clothes. Not dry. Stern, it's tossing, unhooks the canvas, looks at the sky, red. Too bright to get their bearings. Night soon. An afternoon or a day and a half have passed. Almost no wind. Around, water—water.

She's doing better. She's already doing better. The tot watches her scrutinizing. He shuts his eyes. He hears her close the awning. Feels her slide beside him. Feels her take the amauti back in her arms. To fall back asleep immediately. A racket wakes them—above them. Immediately the waves rise in crests. Search for something to hold onto, slide, roll, crash—with one arm, she still holds, squeezed against her breast, the amauti. While the tot stands up with difficulty, she is already looking through the slits in the canvas at the raft—white light, bright sky, these waves. She puts the amauti in his arms, rushes to the stern, detaches the canvas, watches now, standing. She shouts something. The canvas claps, intermittently he sees, not watches, how her legs appear and disappear, squeezes the amauti, in his throat, a knot. Light, shadow, light, sky—bright, sun over the horizon, clap, legs, shadow, light, legs. Bends over, she rifles through the crates. He watches her. He smells her. A place. That was a plane. We must not be far from a coast, it wouldn't be flying so low. We have to shoot off flares. I'm going to shoot off flares. She continues rifling through the crates, gathering anything necessary, turns towards him, tries to catch his eye. I'm going to fire the flares. Take care of the baby. She lowers the awning, disappears. The firing-off of a first, then a second. Nothing. Not more. Nothing magical, if they've been located, it will take some time for someone to come get them. Now to wait. Hesitates over firing a third. Height, brightness, diffraction, and reflection— useless. Now, to relax again. Same gestures, again. Slips under the canvas, takes the tot's temperature, his forehead to hers. The temperature starts dropping. She gives him medicine again. Takes the amauti back in her arms. Hands the kid a can of water. He is able to drink on his own. She cradles the baby, sings in hushed tones. *Oky toky unga.* Looks at her, says nothing. *Oky toky unga / hey misha, dey misha, do misha dey / hexa coola misha, hexa coola misha.* Falls asleep. Oky *toky unga, oky toky unga / hey miska, dey misha, do misha dey / hexa coola misha, hexa coola misha.* She can't sit still

anymore, although she was just ready to fall back asleep. She puts the amauti in the kid's arms. Goes to feel the clothes. Not dry yet. Have to wait. Have to wait now. Watches them, hums, *oky toky unga / hey misha, dey misha, do misha dey / hexa coola misha, hexa coola misha*. Hushes up, decides to go out, takes the driest t-shirt, *oky toky unga*, goes back to the stern, looks for the binoculars, finds them, leaves the shelter, keeps humming, *oky toky unga / hey misha, dey misha* . . . She scans the horizon instead of going back into the tent. *Oky toky unga, oky toky unga / hey misha, dey misha, do misha dey*, the hours pass, *hexa coola misha, hexa coola misha* . . . Thanks to the crest of a wave, she can see the mountaintops disappearing. Reappearing. Disappearing again. Reappearing again. The oars! Paddle now, go meet the shore: she rushes inside, the canvas claps, daylight inside the shelter, the tot awake in the light and, beside him, the amauti. She stares at the kid. Words and hands flow, run together. Take care of the baby. Take it in your arms, cradle it while. While. We have to be able to make land. Take care of the baby while I row. It might be our only chance before the current drags us off again. She doesn't wait for an answer. Unfastens the oars. Leaves. The kid hears her shout, we're gonna get out of here!, then the sound of the oars as they slap the water. As they slap the water. Slap. The mountainous crests block out the horizon. Brown, green. Slap. *Oky toky unga*—raging. The beach appears over the top of the waves. *Oky toky unga*. Slap. We're almost there! And. Again. Oky toky. Short breath. Slap. Again. Again. *Oky. Toky. Unga.* Again. *Toky.*
Oky. Toky. Unga. Again.
Slap. Again. Unga.
And,
she leaps over the side of the raft, drags it, stoops, drags, to dry land, on the beach, drags, last effort, saved, collapses exhausted.

They surround her, without speaking, when she wakes up. First, their movements all around, some bird calls nearby, further away the backwash. The wind, light, warm, intermittent, the sun and some shade. She opens her eyes. Brown canvas over her head. Across, sun and shadow—some trees. Children's faces, some smiling, others interrogating her. The beach, the sand under her fingers, her thighs, laid out on the sand, hot, dry, not very far from the sea, the backwash, the birds, at the edge of the forest laid out under a canvas awning—by these children? Her eyes squinting, sits up on an elbow, tries to look around. The sun blinds her over the shade of the shelter. She asks them, where are we? Some are standing still, staring at her, others shake their hands, speak amongst themselves. She doesn't understand what they express; their hand gestures are different than those she and the tot use. She wants to sit up, dizziness, is forced to lie back down. She looks at the shadow and light on the canvas. Lifts her arms, over her chest, her hands, and again, where are they? They surround her, dense, hide the beach from her. Sees nothing, just all these children around her, shaking. In good health. High cheeks. Clean. Shorts, t-shirts, sandals. One of them hands her something to drink, in a plastic receptacle. She sniffs. Water, just water. A girl makes an encouraging motion. If they had wanted—before. When the huntress-gatheress bows her arms to mimic the gesture of cradling a baby, the children scatter in an instant. In the time it takes her to stand, for her vision to grow used to the sun, to the reflection of the light on the sand, beyond the shade of the shelter, they disappear. Sand, rounded overhang, water—the sea about sixty feet away. No other shelter but the one she is under. On the beach, no trace of the raft, the tot, or the baby. Looking to the right, the left, sees no other shelter but the one she is under, no hut—some sand, the sea. On the beach, no trace of the raft, the tot, or the baby—this sand jetty in the sea means nothing to her. It's not there. The huntress-gatheress tries to find what could have caused this movement—animal? human? Nothing. Some wind. The birds behind her. Squatting, leaves the shelter. Picks herself up carefully. Looks ahead, right, left, behind. Sees, above the silhouette of the trees, some towers of buildings, barely rising above. No new vertigo. No apparent—immediate— danger. Takes the canvas that was sheltering her, tears it. Rolls a piece of it around her head, another around her body. Ties, tightens. Undoes the two sticks over which the canvas was stretched. Knocks them against one another. Dry. Intact. Tough. First weapons. She looks at the ground—the bowl from which she drank, a bottle of water. Gathers them. All around too many tracks in every direction. Trampled ground. It leads to the sea. The huntress-gatheress walks in these footsteps—straight, forward, toward the sea. The wet sand is already smooth. They must have run along the fringe of the waves. Impossible to know where they came from, where they went—right, left? Goes back. Forest. Buildings. Mountains. Remembers the shape of their peak's line when she was rowing. Has to go to the left, she made land further to the left. She walks. Encounters no one but sees freight ships crossing the horizon. How could they not have been fished up? Finds, after several miles, how much time?, she doesn't know, maybe half an hour?, parallel tracks going from the sea to the forest; a heavy object was dragged over this distance. The raft? Nothing was left behind on the beach. The huntress-gatheress follows the tracks—the threshold of the forest. The raft is there, orange in the middle of the green, turned over, pressed against a tree whose trunk is surrounded by necklaces made of little white shells, feathers, plastic pearls. The raft set out to dry in the shade—so the sun wouldn't destroy the plastic? To the side, the huntress-gatheress recognizes, under the tarp of the tent, the angles formed by the crates; placed like this, the tarp protects them and makes them seem one, one entity, one property. She lifts, inspects: the crates have been sorted, organized, closed, piled.

She checks what was left behind. Rational sample of the objects they were transporting. A bit of everything was taken and everything is left—equipment, weapons, food, water, medical kit. Some of their clothes, dry, folded. A path plunges into the forest. It doesn't make sense: she, several miles away, the raft here, which didn't suffer any real pillaging. The kid, if he'd been in the right shape, might have been able to organize it, the things, like this. But he's not there, he didn't leave behind any of the agreed-upon signs. None of the hints she taught him to leave, no hint—blending into the environment, legible to her. Tries to remember. The plane. The mountain, the horizon. She's rowing. *Oky. Toky.* Under the tent, the kid hardly conscious, the amauti in his arms. He and the baby, where? The kid, the amauti in his arms. Too weak to protect himself, them. Too weak. Where were they taken—by whom? Who separated them, her, the tot, the baby? The children who waited for her to wake up, who gave her something to drink?—who disappeared. Would they have been able to drag the raft, put it somewhere dry, sort everything, organize it? They had nothing—nothing in their hands, except this bowl, a bottle of water. Nothing from the raft—nothing seen in their hands, their arms, which would have been taken from the raft. Out of eyeshot, before she got up, others who could have? There are these buildings noticed a moment ago, and this path that sinks into the forest. The birds chatter in the trees. Under the raft, in the raft, something? She slides in. Nothing, if not underneath, the dirt turned over, loose, black, moist. On her knees, the huntress-gatheress feels the dirt. She takes a fistful, kneads it, pulls the seeds from it, inhales it—greasy, sticky, claylike. Intended for the kid, on the bottom of the raft, inside, she uses the dirt to draw a line where they had been lying. So he knows, if he isn't far, that she passed by here. She goes back out from the raft's cover. Moisture, the forest, and dry wind compete, coming from the beach. She's hungry. Eats a boxful, observes her surroundings, sitting on the crates, from the beach to the forest. She listens. Occasionally a muted rumble, the stifled and distant noise of engines, background noise drowning out the birds' sharp cries. And yet no one walks by. The freight ships keep streaming past, minuscule, on the horizon. No fishermen—no boats. She opts for the forest—beyond the forest, these buildings. Cut through. Find them. She puts back the box, empty, where she found it. Slips into a t-shirt, thick leggings, too hot, meant for the winter—she thinks, the insects, I don't know the insects, leggings could be useful. A belt. Puts on shoes. Arm herself? Lightly, arm herself lightly—arm herself, a knife, the switchblade, short, for carving, if a path needs to be carved out over the one that seems to be there. Her P38, loaded, slipped into her belt. One of the sticks. No backpack for transporting further ammunition, reserves. Can return here, yes. Wipes away the tracks she has made. Starts on the path. It snakes between the trees, and soon, between the trees, marshes. Forward. Salty humours of the bayou—corrosive. Mosquitos. That no one has come here, passed by chance—understandable. But this path, traced, worked—very little, a thin thread. These children around her? Across, on the beach, too much. City-dwellers. Not from the forest, knowing the beach. Their footsteps disappeared on the fringe of the backwash. Past the bayou, the murmur of the city. Becomes omnipresent. The huntress-gatheress moves away from the path, hodgepodge of branches, lianas, leaves, undergrowth, living and dead, stick held in front, brushes aside, weaving, a solid tree, tall, climbs, observes. Between the trunks appears a narrow clearing, where corrugated iron, boards stand together—households. Between, shadows slide. Observes exchanges, clothing. Comings and goings. Women and men. Teenagers and adults. Leaving or arriving, bringing or taking something away. Lots of activity. Young children play on the ground, in front of the doors, or further off, scattered— in bunches. Older ones keep an eye on them from far away, pass by, move away, return, disappear—sometimes; the children who surrounded her when she woke up did not come from here. Old women and men, sitting, together, discuss—out of earshot. Chants— monotone. Flutes. Attentive to the children. Smoke from the fires with pots hung over them, the wind carries appetizing smells—stews, spices. Toward the city, border of scooters, bikes, cars, a truck—rusted, patched up. It's organized. Viable. No aggression. She observes them. Thinks of QANNAC. Her communities. XINGPING, son amour. The steppes, how they hunted. To find son amour. Save herself, them. The straight line from Greenland to the center of China. White and gray. Cracks in the ice shelf. JAN MAYEN, the coiling smoke. The volcano. To find the baby and the tot. Departure. Arrival. There, where? Observes, scans the children to see if the tot and baby are with them. Maybe, too weak, they could be in one of the cabins? Wonders if it's the children she sees who pulled the raft, sorted the crates, how she got so far from where they made landfall, who these children are, surrounding her, if the ones she sees know something. She watches them. Discussions, exchanges, games, chants—peaceful. Endless comings and goings. Looks at the buildings through the foliage of the trees. Go over there directly, avoiding those down below? Go down, ask them? Meet them unarmed? Sigh. Start somewhere. Concentrates. Choose intuitively. The movements of her heart. The wind tosses the treetop from which she observes—the encampment?, the village? A birdsong. Another one answers. A woman sees her watching, motions for her to join her. Incapable of not being detected? If they are as peaceful as they seem, then. Then, what? How to find out? Are they going to come for her, make her climb down, question her? The woman gestures again. The huntress-gatheress doesn't respond. Can still flee. Avoid them. A man arrives, same height as the woman, tells her something, the woman listens to him, answers, doesn't point her out, doesn't indicate her presence to the man. They turn away. They leave together. Opposite direction from her, toward the city. Are they going to find someone to—arrest her? The huntress-gatheress waits.

---

1 - Notebook of the huntress-gatheress, pp. 110, 111-113, 117, 130-140, 142-147.
2 - *Ibid.*, pp. 118-119.

Nothing. Her presence, known, nothing changes in anyone's activities. Trap? She is tired—her mistrust. Goes down, and starts on the path that leads to the encampment. Hesitates. Still to spy on them, approach them, listen, watch, try to surprise them if something is brewing against her. One of them knows she is there. Hesitates. To disarm herself, go like that into the clearing of their encampment, in sight, hands up. Hesitates. To go back to the canoe. Hesitates while bypassing the village to make it to the city. Squats on the path. What to do? There is this fear. In her gut, this fear. A few yards off—a birdsong, the same as the one she has heard, though on top of a tree. Another melody answers it, from the other side of the path. She watches. Sees a silhouette between the trees. Someone observes her—calm. Turns her head, sees someone else. Turns her head, the other one has disappeared. Turns her head. No one. Stands up. If they're observing her like that, these people must know something—that woman gesturing to her. Wants her to go to them. The village, a few dozen yards away. Trap or not? She is tired. Makes up her mind. Ready to fight if. When she goes in, no one assaults her—no mob. The ones who see her, nod to her. Nobody seems threatened by her presence. An old man rises and welcomes her, as she saw other adults being welcomed. He speaks quickly, without stopping, she doesn't understand, he leads her slowly to the group where he was sitting. It seems they're talking about her, they give her a place, sit her with them. She lets it happen. Listens. Doesn't understand. An teenager brings a platter—of fruits, she doesn't recognize their shapes. Automatically notes—what to gather, edible. He leaves, comes back, gives everyone a bowl—inside, something to eat, one of the stews she could smell. She receives one. She observes the gestures around her. The bowls are exchanged. A leather gourd, passed from hand to hand—water. Everyone eats, she imitates them.

---

3 - Notebook of the huntress-gatheress, pp. 124-125.

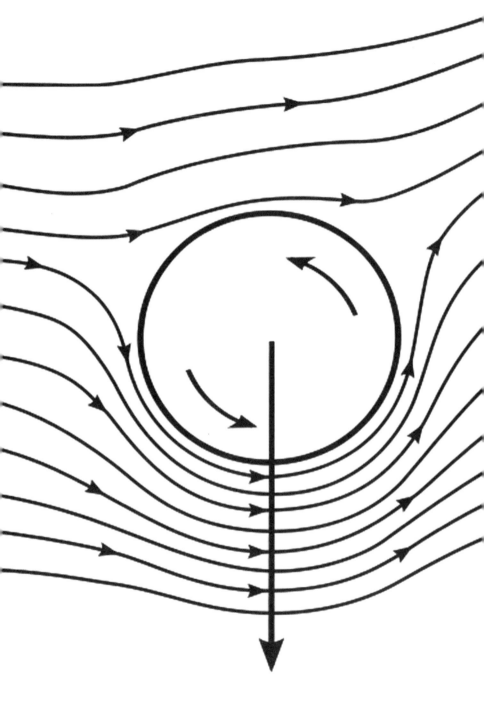

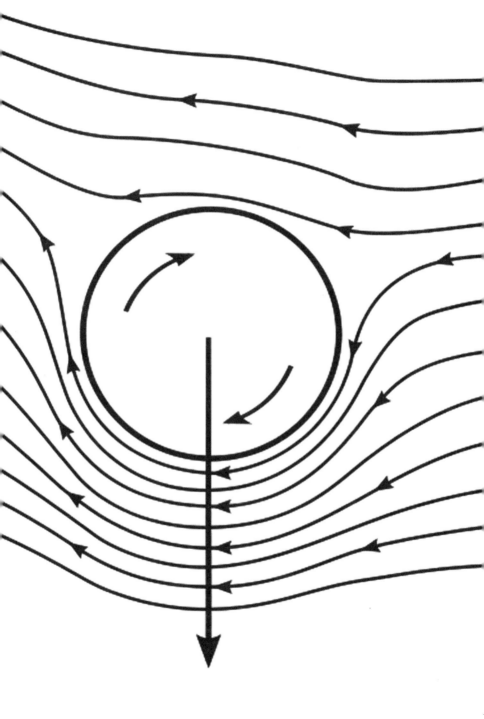

Amongst themselves, they speak, occasionally addressing her—alternate between languages. Until she can understand, can speak. Do you understand? They agree, smiling. Yes. You can take rest here. Continue their discussions amongst themselves, not really addressing her, dealing with factual things, mixing their voices, interventions of someone or other, one, several, a woman, a man, together, anecdotes, recipes, agreements, accounts, laughter, cuentos de camino, everyday, memories, neither include nor exclude her. Their language changes again. Occasionally an adult comes to see them, asks some questions and leaves again. She observes. After having changed several times more, their language comes back to hers. She asks them where she is. In Nicaragua. Between Granada and Rivas. Not far from the beaches of the Bay of Nicaragua. The Bay of Nicaragua? The lake turned into a bay. There is a second passage now between the Atlantic and Pacific. The one the Americans wanted. At last, they have it. Not what they imagined, but they have it. They did it. Now there's a passage. Parallel to Panama. Or almost. On other side, Costa-Rica-Panama island. The two Americas are separate. Officially. As of a few weeks ago. A few weeks? Yes, a few weeks. Then it's been . . . I wanted to get to China by way of the Arctic. We set out from Greenland. We'd been rolling for a few days. We were making good progress. The ice shelf gave way. We ended up near an island. JAN MAYEN. There was an eruption. Then we drifted, I guess we drifted. We? The kid, the baby, our dog, and I. On a raft. All the way here. I woke up later, without the kid or the baby. Dzeta died after the eruption. I had to throw her into the sea. Was it you who carried me here? No. I found the raft. The kid and baby weren't there. Someone set the raft out to dry. At the edge of the forest. That's where I came from. The path leads here. You didn't see anything? The raft, yes, we found it. There was a baby inside. Wrapped in furs. They go quiet. The old man who led the group takes her hand. She looks at them. Dizzy.

The kid wakes up in a white bed, a dormitory. No sounds. Alone. It's day out. Birdsongs in the trees, their shadows in the room, their silhouettes on the white curtains drawn over the window, open, above the bed where he lies. He remembers the faces of the children surrounding him as they accosted him on the beach. His body isn't in pain. He lifts his hands, certain fingers wrapped in bandages. He gets up carefully. Nothing. No sharp pain. Dressed—underwear, t-shirt. One step to the window. Sun misted out. Aggressive humidity. A courtyard surrounded by buildings. Leans in, listens. The birds. The wind in the trees. Their leaves. Some windows, all open, very little sound. Only a few snatches of speech, muffled, make it to him. Goes back to the room. Long. Doors at both ends. Two facing rows of beds. Each one, made with clean sheets, sits below a double casement window. He crosses the room. Faces window, leans on his elbows, looks, leans. In the distance, the flat surface of the sea—the ocean, some body of water. Underscored by—narrow strip, thin, green, forest. Then, grey, a city. Further down, a city. Green ribbon, another forest separates the buildings— hardly thick, a park? From here, this overhang—sea, forest, city, forest. He goes back to the room. Next to the bed where he was sleeping, on the nightstand, clothes. His, a pair of shorts. On the floor, sandals. He gets dressed. Considers going through the other nightstands to find something useful for self-defense. In the end, leaves through a door almost directly across from him. A hallway. No one. And yet the building isn't empty, he heard it—now feels it. A stairway gives onto the courtyard he could see from the dormitory. Find someone? Knock on one of the doors? Wait? Some children found him. Apparently brought him here, he's doing ok. Wait. He knows how to wait. He waits. Looks at the leaves. Looks at the birds. Some birds he has never seen before. The leaves. The rustling. The wind. The rustling. The water. The noise of the waves. The waves. JAN MAYEN.

An old woman clucks her tongue against the roof of her mouth. The huntress-gatheress looks at her and, where is the baby? The old woman goes quiet. Where is the baby? We buried it. Under the raft. The dirt turned over, my hand, the black dirt, the sign—the huntress-gatheress chokes, closes her eyes, wants to leave, stands up, is held back by the old man's hand—its pressure, and two hands her shoulders down, sit her down, a young woman, her two hands, without violence, with strength, push down on the huntress-gatheress' shoulders, murmurs, stay with us. The baby. Its grave. I want to go. I want to be sure. I want. The elders start to sing, quietly. Her hand, still in the old man's. Let me go. Stay with us. Later, you'll go. For now stay with us. Passed from hand to hand, a bowl. Continue the songs. Everyone drinks—one sip. Makes it to her. Hesitates. Looks at the old man, drinks, the crouching woman, her face, her hand—staying there, holding her, seated. Drinks. Hesitates. The songs—circulate, circle, chorus without center, turn, drink again, here, there, there, here, there, and. Dizziness. Lets go. Drinks. Some children join them, post up behind them, take their places, rest their heads on their knees—some of them have even smaller children in their arms. The gestures are sweet, slow, calm. Welcomed. The songs interrupted. The children speak amongst themselves, in hushed tones, murmur, songs beneath songs. Certain ones imitate those who are singing, join the melodies, speech, intonations—offer their modulating voices, their rhythms, babble. Not harmonized so much as made heard, but everyone goes on, together, singing more important than song. Dizziness. Closes her eyes. Dizziness multiplied—space, full, hollow, other. Wants to leave. Unable. Songs. Circle. Songs. A baby cries. Songs in the huntress-gatheress' closed eyes. Snow. Ice. Soft furs. Way over there. Humming-birds. The river. Its bends. Shores, pebbles, sands, gravel. Songs. Explosions, engines. Snow. Melts.

Dzeta between his legs. No doubt he killed her by suffocating her—his legs, too tight, hold her. Would have struggled. Dead from fear? The impact of a rock, of an ice block that didn't tear the canvas? No doubt he killed her. The dead baby. The crazy face of the huntress-gatheress when she doesn't see the baby. Doesn't want to see it. Where is she? The children must know. He will ask them. Maybe. Maybe he will have to flee. Wait. Not to wander in the building without knowing where he is, for how long has he been there. Under whose watch? A bell. Some children come out, fill up the courtyard. Noises of their movements, absence of their voices. They heckle each other—don't notice him. He observes them. One. Two, several realize they are being spied on. Sitting, scans, waits. Moves forward. Calm, still. Near. Stands up, slowly. Be slow. Know how to be slow. They speak to him with their hands. Some of them articulate a few words, like punctuation of what is said. He doesn't understand. They use signs he doesn't know. Very fast. And when they speak, he doesn't understand it either. He makes a first sign. He mimes a first sign. Walk. Speak. The children converse amongst themselves. It's very fast. They stop. Come back to him. And use another language. Not his, either. But slower and simpler. A boy. Do you understand now? Yes. Another boy. Are you ok? Yes. A girl. Did you get some rest? Yes. The questions come one after the other, simple, posed by turns by each of the children there, fifteen or so. A young man approaches their group. He speaks to the boy in the same language the children have decided to use to speak to him. This language seems to come more naturally to the young man than to the children. A little slower, a young girl informs him. She continues, it's not the same as ours; he understands but it has to be slower. The young man smiles at him, agrees. Says to the kid, I work here; this place is a, the kid doesn't understand, for; welcome; would you like to come with me so I can introduce you to, once again the kid doesn't understand.

This baby who still didn't have a first name, the baby to whom a first name still hadn't been given, her breathing steadies, not yet old enough to be given a first name, a baby who didn't survive. Dead from bruising, dead from cold, dead from hunger? Dead. Face contorted—eyes, mouth closed, cries without tears. Sees the baby, its smiles, crying, silences. Its movements, suckling, games, sleep. Its birth. Her pregnancy. The father. She will have to tell the father the baby is dead. She cries as she knows how to cry—with eyes closed. The old man's hand holds hers, bringing her back, gently, into the songs, with them, everyone, children and elders. Her face toward the ground—eyes closed, cries. The songs go on. The hand held by the old man. His answer. His hand. He smiles at her gently, all while speaking words she cannot understand. Cries—eyes closed. A child's voice, close to the old man, sings, brightly—standing behind. Cries—eyes closed, no tears, the face, strained. Wants to leave. Stay. Wants to stay— to forget. Wants to leave—to see. Hands on her shoulders. The bright song. The old voice. The beaten earth, squealing, a centipede crawls—her foot. Absence. The hands keeping the song's rhythm, caress, slide, the wind. Cries—her face. A tongue clucks in a mouth—tongue, roof. Cluck. Wind, rubbing, caresses, their hands keeping rhythm. Songs. Face, dirt—cries. Her face, straining, cries. Hand, hand, songs. The child's bright voice, standing, behind. The old man's, joined with the others. Songs. A tongue clucks in a mouth— tongue, roof. You can take rest here. Tasha will show you. Songs. Hands keep rhythm, caress, slide, the wind. His hand, her hand. Her face, strained. Cries—her face. The hands on her shoulders have disappeared. The bright song. His hand in her hand has disappeared. The bright voice and the songs. Tasha will go with you. Opens. She obeys. The old man's child with the bright voice comes to her. Come. Come with me.

He looks at the other children. Smile at him. Are they encouraging him? He looks again at the young man. Ok. I'll come. The kid approaches the young man, who starts to walk. The kid follows him, turning away. The children say see you soon. They cross the courtyard, opposite from where he woke up. If the young man watches him from time to time, kindly, makes sure he is being followed, adds nothing. Arrived before a massive door, wood, glass, old, a hall, he pulls it open, holds it, the kid enters, the young man follows him. Points out a hallway to the right. Row of doors. The young man walks ahead of him again, walks up to one of them. Opens it, moves aside, invites the tot in. The kid, slow, slow-willed, joins him, while he crosses the threshold, the young man tells him he will be back shortly and, once the tot has entered, closes the door again—slowly. Thickness of the carpeting. The tot freezes. In the room, several people, women and men, coats, pleated pants, straight skirts, standing, mid-conversation, their hands wave, or, sitting in armchairs, behind desks, write by hand, type on keyboards. Tranquility. The birds, still, in the trees—the windows open, and the wind, the damp. Silence of slowness, clicking of the muffled bolt. A woman approaches the kid, asks him would you like to sit?, have something to drink? Same simple signs as the young man. No—expression, head motion. Do you know where you are? Shrug. A school. A little more than a school adds a man. The woman resumes saying a school for, the tot doesn't understand, deaf-mutes. The kid makes up his mind, tries—their language, adapt his, some what?, can you make that sign again? Children who no longer have mothers or fathers. She makes the sign again, aloud *huérfano*. You speak? You, you hear. She smiles and adds as for me I can't hear my voice; are you talking? Not yet. Oh, I see. She is still smiling, raises an eyebrow. The kid isn't sure he knows what she sees, but gives a hint of a smile—smile, the huntress-gatheress. How did I get here. A, he doesn't understand, on the beach. He gestures again.

The huntress-gatheress gets up, the child takes her by the hand. An old man clicks his tongue on the roof of his mouth. She looks at him. Follow Tasha. The child hardly makes it up to her waist and pulls her out of the circle of women and men singing. Move away, the songs continue. To go see if. The songs, the child, Tasha. To leave to see if. Stay. Wait. The songs. The huntress-gatheress is of three minds. The songs, her legs, her stomach and her heart, her face, cries, and the songs. Wants to leave, go back to the raft, or the songs. Arrives at the threshold of a hut of corrugated iron and boards. Over the ground of beaten earth, the child stops and steps aside—lets her in. The huntress-gatheress, the raft, the songs, the raft, the grave, the baby, relax. Tasha is going to go with you, relax, wants to leave, wants to run, can't. Tasha sits at the threshold, the huntress-gatheress still standing, same place. Shuts her eyes. Opens. Turns. Turns toward the path. A few seconds running for. Toward the circle, a few dozen steps. Toward the inside. Dark. Wants, calm down. Standing. Makes out the inside. Goes in. On the ground, a pile of several covers. A plastic bowl and a clay bowl side by side. Each filled. Her daikyu. her quiver and arrows. Toward the child, at the threshold. Sitting at the threshold. Sits down. Beaten earth, silky. The child's face turned toward the song. The kid's face across from the face of the dead baby. The dead baby's face in the amauti. The face. Her strained face, cries. Leave to see. Her weapons. Her anger. The baby. Her anger. Leave. Barks at Tasha, am I a prisoner? Tasha shrugs her shoulders, sullen pout, and looks outside again. Do you speak my language? Tasha looks at her again then turns her face away, indifferent, toward the outside. The huntress-gatheress looks as though she is leaving. Immediately Tasha turns and lifts her palm, forbidding it. Were you waiting for me? Tasha lifts her eyebrows and doesn't answer. She would like to sleep, cry, leave, talk. Strength gone. She lies down, beaten earth. To sleep. Shuts her eyes. Her face strained. Fights. The songs continue. The baby dead, the kid missing. Dzeta devoured, the baby dead, the kid missing.

Adds an interrogative. *Excursion.* He nods. An excursion. Did you also bring her here? Who? The woman who was with me? You didn't find her? She wasn't with me? No. The children found you alone. In the raft? She gestures uncertainly. I don't know exactly. I wasn't with them. They said they found you on the beach, passed out. Alejandro and Béthel weren't with them at that instant. Since you were burning up Alejandro and Béthel decided to come back here right away so a doctor could take a look at you. Where are you from? The north. The north? What north? Where it's cold. If I show you a map can you show me? Of course. Come with me. She heads to a computer and sits down. After a moment, she shows him a map of the world. The kid's face scrunches up. What is it? The map is different. The woman lets out a sigh. Yes. The kid points to a blue area in the north. That's where I come from. How did you get here? By sea. You were saying that you were accompanied by someone? Yes. There were four of us. Her, the baby, Dzeta, and me. Dzeta? Our dog. She's dead. The baby's also dead. She looks at him, trying to stay calm—to keep smiling, her face freezing up. She turns toward the other people in the room. Everyone has more or less followed the exchange. They motion to her to keep going. All right; I'm going to ask the children who found you to come in, when they're done with class. Do you know where you were going? The kid nods, points to another place at the heart of China. Can you show me where we are? She shows him Managua, Nicaragua. The kid traces with his finger a course going from Qaanaaq drowned by the dismantled ice shelf, straight to the North Pole, passing by JAN MAYEN. All the way to Nicaragua. We must have done something like that. She looks again at the others, inquiringly. Some gestures. Randy is going to take you to visit the school. Randy? The young man who came to get you in the courtyard; my name is Bitsie, and you? He makes a complicated hand gesture.

Having wanted to leave, to save herself, to save them, to have lost them all. To have lost everything. The baby dead. The baby's face in the amauti. Its eyes closed. The rigidity of, this cold, the colors of. The baby's face. The amauti entrusted to the kid. The tot's crazy eyes when, the paddles, stroke, the paddles. Gone—mad, gone? The kid turning down the amauti. The dead baby's face. The stillness of its face. The baby dead against her back. The baby dead in the amauti. The baby dead. The kid missing. Her, further still from what she wanted to join again. It's me who killed my people. It's me who killed my people, my people, the baby and the tot. Tasha looks at her from time to time, but more drawn to what is happening outside, turns away quickly, uninterested. The old women and men asked her to keep watch by the doorway of the hut. This woman laid out on the ground. Shaking. Whose lips quiver. Who stays there, who wants to leave and stay. When night falls, a younger adult joins Tasha, he talks to her, questions her, then sits down and takes her in his arms. Now there are two with their backs to the doorframe, at times looking outside, the fires glowing between the huts, around the circle formed by the old women and men, at times listening to the huntress-gatheress. Night falls and Tasha falls asleep in the man's arms. Night passes and the man falls asleep. In the morning an old woman joins them, one of the ones who had spoken to the huntress-gatheress the night before. After a few words to Tasha and the young man, the old woman steps over them and comes in. The huntress-gatheress does not react. The old woman sits down beside her. In her palm, some knucklebones, which she throws down between them. Rattling at consistent intervals. The huntress-gatheress is still, her eyes turned toward the woven straw. In one of the old woman's hands rattle the knucklebones, the other is resting on the huntress-gatheress' forehead. Rattling. Bony hand on the huntress-gatheress' forehead, the old woman, in hushed tones, bursts into song, a cuento de camino, and sings:

Bitsie repeats awkwardly, uncertainly, adds an interrogative. He reproduces his gesture and adds I can't explain that. Randy comes into the room, places himself before the tot, smiling, still. Let's go? Yes. She adds pay attention to him. The signs she makes are ambiguous—protection and observation. Randy takes the tot by the shoulder. Which immediately shrinks away. The young man feels it, lets go of his hand. Excuse me. I'm going to bring you to visit the orphanage, all right? Yes. Brief head motions are exchanged between Randy and Bitsie. From the others to Randy. Which the tot watches. Interprets. Randy turns back toward the kid. Let's go? Ok. Bitsie accompanies them to the door, which she opens for them and closes behind them—the kid hears her sigh, the door whooshes. They go down the same path again. Here, the courtyard where the children play between classes; you were going to school? Randy watches the tot. Who reflects, the most adapted response, something the huntress-gatheress taught him, the others, alone—yes. Randy explains everything around, the classrooms, the children are inside them right now. His arm points to the first floor of the building to their right, there's the library. The tot nods. Randy turns back toward the door through which they had just left. Here, the administration. Do you understand this word? Administration. The tot nods. Not very comfortable with this word, Randy notes. Turns back, points to the second floor of the building whose length faces them. There, that's where the children sleep, the dormitory where you woke up—the kid makes the gesture again, dormitory. Below, where we eat, the cafeteria. Gesture repeated by the tot. They cross the courtyard, enter the building, narrow, walk through it, come out almost immediately onto a terrace, wide, of stone. At a height just above the foliage of the trees, certain ones entirely white, the tot distinguishes the flowers covering them, beyond, down below, the city stretches out, beyond, still green and then the sea. View almost the same as the one from the dormitory. From the terrace, an imposing stairway whose last steps are hidden by the trees. The terrace wraps around the building. Randy points to him in this direction,

lever du soleil,
lever comme l'est,
sun rising, ensuite,
lever est l'ouest,
the sun just rose,
it's nice out
the weather,
comes, in the first
place, to start up a
conversation, and at
times shut it down,
nothing left but it,
letting everything be
said, joy as sadness,
with great modesty,
completely in secret
in the meadow,
the morning
frost of the past
months become,
on that morning,
simple dew,
n a d a — d e w
Roa's gift the
multitudes of junctions
become traps
A branch breaks
craque in the
chestnut tree
in bloom,
white flowers,
hiding the
memory of the
fuschia ones.

GOING
FAIR

the threshold whose strength is the heart,
its output, its sweetness and fury
heard, all in knots and carried away,
flags me down, the days passing in our footsteps,

nowhere is my country today
i've been banished from the one that,
whose trees have disappeared,
far from here and now,

cedars, birches, baobabs, beeches,
oaks, lindens, cherries, weeping willows,
some evening the earth,
dry and humid, acidic, alkaline,
neutral,

all the trees are
from now on of my country
we go toward, and toward

we don't know what we'll find for ourselves
the days passing in our footsteps
as the passing forests, plains, mountains, and banks
and the beaches, bare and discovered, to be discovered;

at the river's threshold, where a fossilized whale,
its baleen of stone, its granite organ
leaves us fragile at the feet of its sheer face

find, before the night, the vital refuge,
some men and women,
fire,
they insist, and take us back

a wood's edge, then the woods, in the hunting blind

from the woods the noises are immense,
terrifying, bestial, beasts and men, women and chimeras,
barbarians, possible,
possible,

the forest, the undergrowth,
the chiaroscuro, the diagonal mounting
of light and insects,
incantations to, what do I know,

fear rises
from, what do I know; that's what fear is
in the hunting blind
and, those four
protect me,

we walk, and
I, trumpets & songs, invisible, we rise, the light falls,
and from the inert bodies of my companions, their voices,
united, over
a single chord, are still, cry and call to me, I
rise up, hear them disappearing

the threshold whose strength is the heart,
its output, its sweetness and fury
heard, all in knots and carried away,
flags me down, the days passing in our footsteps,

I,
in the air, suspended, walk,
like I've never walked before

feeling the ground that is not,
any longer, beneath my feet,
I

above the forest
the forest given to my eye, dizziness, dizziness
of the mountains, of the unspooling plains, and
I walk, the stars I touch them
and the moon and

I walk until morning
in the rocky and twinkling silence
of the stars
until
until I reach where
we are given back to each other
I'm there, in a night,
arrival
arrived,

the threshold whose strength is the heart,
its output, its sweetness and fury
heard, all in knots and carried away,
flags me down, the days passing in our footsteps,

in the freezing air, her breath
allows me to see her, the mist and the light,
born in the east, of the sun,
slit it, uncover it,
gaseous and watery,
veil, open, fold, and drape
the elsewhere the nowhere and the unknown.

the mysterious night, where does it come from,
fly off to, powdery, the beaten earth of the path,
it moves ahead, clarifies
its demand, he asks her, asks me to
come find her, come here, where she stays
motionless in movement,

approaches, toward me,
knowing of me that it's me
her hand on my shoulder and her smile,
which comes to find her, to lead her away,
the outer wall surpassed, the city, through,
sleeping, its details craggy
in the frosty morning air,
to the house of who,
of the one who, my master's,
where my old master jaguar,
waits, awaits her,
silently

silently, we
in the city, walk on toward,
what she knows, what she doesn't know,
silently, we arrive
before
where it
awaits him, where, the threshold surpassed, only she goes in

the threshold whose strength is the heart,
its output, its sweetness and fury
heard, all in knots and carried away,
flags me down, the days passing in our footsteps,

an alligator-woman
a hummingbird-man
a spider-monkey-man
a deer-woman
a boa-man
a toucan-woman
sitting at the table, stare me down,
mute

stare each other down, mute, and with a
single movement, together show
me the stairs, order me,
jointly, to climb it,
walk
after
walk
after
walk
after
walk
after
walk
after
walk
after
the landing
the door

the threshold whose strength is the heart,
its output, its sweetness and fury
heard, all in knots and carried away,
flags me down, the days passing in our footsteps,

ajar, through the doorframe I'm embraced
by master jaguar's den, his backlit silhouette, his other side, his back,
invisible face facing the window, his hands folded low,
he watches and listens to the river's
grunts
in which his own eddy
around, his naked jaguarian face: come in

the threshold whose strength is the heart,
its output, its sweetness and fury
heard, all in knots and carried away,
flags me down, the days passing in our footsteps,

approaching, the woman
I was waiting for, arrived, at last, there,
neither outside, nor inside
upright she stands
and hesitates before

busts, pedestals, hands, torsos, faces, moulded bodies, astrolabes, sextants,
octants, compasses, alidades, Jacob's staffs, logs, saphaeas,
great horned owl, ermine, brown bear, raccoon, snakes, meerkats,
stuffed parrots, seashells, stones, lepidopterans and arachnids,
pins, pestles, bowls, platters, plates, money boxes, gemstones, little coins,
pearls, open and closed chests, purses, satchels, sacks of spice,
petals, powders, pigments, herbs gathered, tied, and hung,
potted plants, weeds, catnip, perennials, cultivated plants,
branches of cherry trees, apple trees, peach trees in blossom loaded with
multicolor, colorless, budding flowers, engraved, smooth, full, empty vases
with stagnant water, opaque and translucent bottles with purpurin, violet,
reddish, greenish, piss-yellow, ochre, brownish, syrupy liquids, potions, inks,
paintbrushes, plumes,

skulls, bones, egg shells, anatomic boards rolled up charts and some
unrolled oceans and skies, sea of discarded papers, left on the floor, armor,
daggers, swords, sabers, pistols, muskets, fabrics, wools, furs, velvet,
silks, cottons, white, plain, colorful, with patterns involving everything
that can be found here,

to move toward,
toppling, mid-ellipse,
gravitational, at the half-center
I
stay, she
snakes between, tacks,
wide open her eyes dart toward
me,
soars up

the threshold whose strength is the heart,
its output, its sweetness and fury
heard, all in knots and carried away,
flags me down, the days passing in our footsteps,

we,
us, transported, the immediacy of,
we who don't,
our mouths on our mouths on our faces on
our necks and our shoulders,
resurgent, recognizant,
some
memory pertaining to, to the, there
to those, to our bodies
hugrasping
each other

from, the changing weather, a cloud,
a shower, an eclipse,
the night the day
transported,
transporting us, toppling, topple

the wires, the threads, the
objects
swept into our movement, accompanying,
immediate, nuclear, exploding
on the ground,
us,
on the ground, wrapping each other with
our, us,

impresent pulsatiles,
equational montages
until
no more, we
no more
that what's happening
gives way to us, that we
liquidismiss ourselves

the threshold whose strength is the heart,
its output, its sweetness and fury
heard, all in knots and carried away,
flags me down, the days passing in our footsteps,

happy, so happy,
I gush I flood and flow and flow and flow, I soak the sheets and

spread myself out on the floor, indivisible and divided, I flood and flow and flow between the planks, to the door, under the door, I slide, I snake, I cascade, cascade, cascade, I bound, jump, walk, walk, walk, splash from stair to stair, I mingle with the lime and soak the wood, I cascade and launch, I gush there over a skull, over the astrolabe, there over the U of a half-unrolled map, I soak the paper, the ink runs, a lake is described, cascades

the threshold whose strength is the heart,
its output, its sweetness and fury
heard, all in knots and carried away,
flags me down, the days passing in our footsteps,

I cascade, from stair to stair, cascade, the wax repels me, it splits me, droplets, immiscible I drip, I seep, I gush, I flow, gush, explode, a lake empties out, I'm a lake and a fountain, indivisible and divided, flow, flow, absorbed by the sheets, the blanket, the cotton, I spread out, puddle, at the foot of the stairs, I spread out, I shake under light steps, hands like a conch shell gather me and carry me to the lips, I'm lapped at, drunk up

The voice of the huntress-gatheress joins them then:

the threshold whose strength is the heart,
its output, its sweetness and fury
heard, all in knots and carried away,
flags me down, the days passing in our footsteps,

I am in their throats, I get drunk from the source, I'm on the grating tongue, I go down along the esophagus, I penetrate stomachs, arteries, veins, circulate through blood

the threshold whose strength is the heart,
its output, its sweetness and fury
heard, all in knots and carried away,
flags me down, the days passing in our steps,

I bound, bound, free, gush, bound, I spread out, puddle,
wide puddle, I gather together, seep, droplets in the puddle, I
flow and am absorbed, I steep, I overflow, I moisten skin and
hair, I flood, the walls hold me back, I rise, I rise, I gush

the threshold whose strength is the heart,
its output, its sweetness and fury
heard, all in knots and carried away,
flags me down, the days passing in our footsteps,

I crash down, I cascade, I scare, they run from me, I lick feet, hands,
furniture, flames, fire, I sleet, I evaporate, I extinguish, inside me ash
dilutes, I float, I condense, seep, fall back into
myself, I gush, rise, gush, flow, I jump, fall, absorbed,
held back, I irrigate bodies, I slip between fingers, I get drunk up,
the threshold whose strength is the heart,
its output, its sweetness and fury
heard, all in knots and taken away,
flags me down, the days passing in our steps,
mixed with saliva, saliva dilutes, I am spit out, I gush, I get drunk up,
I cover up, I submerge, I fill, I overflow, liquid firework, I
gurgle, collected I bound into the eye that observes me, I flow from it,
I flood, I cover thighs, stomach, sides, breasts, throat of my source, I run dry,
I ebb, my source falls asleep,

Таблица 45. Ракши:

1 — синебровый момот (Eumomota superciliosa);

2 — обыкновенный зимородок (Alcedo atthis);

3 — золотистая щурка (Merops apiaster);

4 — ямайский тоди (Todus todus).

Off to the side of the building, a hill where, between the trees, small parcels of cultivated land stand out, separated by flowers or berry bushes, laid out in terraces. Gray line, a short building. That one's ours, the tot repeats the sign. Farm, our farm, around us our—our? Gardens. The tot makes the gesture again. Yes. Garden. Where we grow fruits and vegetables, our garden. We grow a bit of everything. That's part of the classes the children take here. Learning how to garden. Learning how to raise livestock. We have three cows, five goats, a donkey, and some turkeys, too. On the other side of the hill, some fields. Around, our park. The orphanage is almost self-sufficient. The children take part in every task. They learn to kill the domesticated animals. Pluck their feathers. Cook them. He turns toward the kid. We're happy to welcome you among us. The tot smiles. Thanks. But I'm not going to stay. Where do you want to go? To find her. Whom? The one I made it to the beach with. Silence. Randy waits for him to say more. He's surprised when the the tot changes the subject and asks him what do you do here? What do you mean? Are you a teacher? No. But you're not like the people in the... administration, either? Are you the person in charge? No, actually not. So what do you do? I take care of the children. Like Alejandro and Béthel; the three of us all do the same thing. Do the children tell you things they wouldn't tell the person in charge? The man notes, out of habit, the progress the child is making; his immediate reuse of terms he hadn't known before, which he makes himself repeat—like the others. Hesitates before saying yes. Adds sometimes. Did they tell you how they found me? Yes. How? The children were walking in groups on the beach. One of them found you there. Unconscious. Feverish. The older ones carried you to the minibus. The younger ones went to find Alejandro and Béthel, the other groups. Since you weren't doing very well, everyone came back here. Fast. Our doctor examined you. Then, you slept. When was that? Two days ago. I slept for two days? Yes. No one's gone back to the beach since? No. Did the children explain where they found me? Pretty far from the road that leads to the beach. By foot? By bus. They were supposed to spend their afternoon over there. Walking around. Observing the sea. Understanding the changes. The map's changes? Yes, the lake became a bay. The two oceans cross in the bay. The beach against the, the tot doesn't understand. The? Randy makes the sign again, explains, from the water, another word the kid doesn't understand, where certain trees grow. He repeats the gesture he hadn't grasped. Randy explains, a mixture of saltwater and freshwater then makes the gesture for brackish again. The kid repeats the first gesture, bayou, marsh, and the second one, brackish. He adds people live over there? Randy seems uncertain, it's a dangerous place. Full of snakes. The kid reflects. All the children who live here are deaf-mutes? Yes; deaf or mute or both. And none has parents? We don't know about everyone, some of them were abandoned, we don't know if their parents are still alive or not. Or if the parents chose to abandon them because they couldn't feed them or didn't know what to do with them, became of their, the tot doesn't understand. Something they couldn't do, which everyone can do, usually. In their case speak or hear. Once again the tot repeats the gesture he sees. Yes. Handicap. The kid stays still. Is everything ok? He shakes his head. Look Randy, the kids I saw just now, I couldn't understand them; they speak a different language? When they arrive, we teach them more or less what we're speaking now, both. Even if you don't understand every little thing, even if there are differences with the one you know, it's close. As for them, the children, they speak a different language amongst themselves. Fabricated from the one we taught them, but faster and with other signs. Do you understand it? I'm more comfortable with the other one. Can you tell me about the plants?

They spend another moment in the garden, then the farm, then Randy and the tot climb to the top of the hill, go down to the fields, walk around there, the tot asks questions, Randy explains things, they continue to the outer wall of the park, follow it, make their way back under the cover of the trees, toward the garden, the orphanage. Randy takes the kid to the library—no one there, aside from the librarian whom Randy asks to keep an eye on the kid—asking the kid to stay until dinner time. He reads and memorizes. Acanthaceae Juss. Achatocarpaceae Heimerl. Actinidiaceae Gilg & Werderm. Agavaceae Dumort. Aizoaceae Martinov. Alismataceae Vent. Amaranthaceae Juss. Anacardiaceae R. By Annonaceae Juss. Apiaceae Lindl. Apocynaceae Juss. Aquifoliaceae Bercht. & J Presl. Araceae Juss. Araliaceae Juss. Arecaceae Bercht. & J Presl. Aristolochiaceae Juss. Asclepiadaceae Borkh. Asteraceae Bercht. & J. Presl. Balanophoraceae Rich. Basellaceae Raf. Bataceae Mart. ex Perleb. Begoniaceae C. Agardh. Betulaceae Gray. Bignoniaceae Juss. Bixaceae Kunth. Bombacaceae Kunth. Boraginaceae Juss. Brassicaceae Burnett. Bormeliaceae Juss. Burnelliaceae Engl. Buddlejaceae K. Wilh. Burmanniaceae Blume. Burseraceae Kunth. Cabombaceae Rich. ex A. Rich. Cactaceae Juss. Caesalpiniaceae R. Br. Campanulaceae Juss. Cannaceae Juss. Capparaceae Juss. Caprifoliaceae Juss. Cariaceae Dumort. Celastraceae R. Br. Ceratophyllaceae Gray. Chenopodiaceae Vent. Chrysobalanaceae R. Br. Cistaceae Juss. Clethraceae Klotzsch. Clusciaceae Lindl. Commelinaceae Mirb. Connaraceae R. Br. Convolvulaceae Juss. Costaceae Nakai. Crassulaceae J. St.-Hil, Cymodoceaceae Vines. Cyperaceae Juss. Cyrillaceae Lindl. Dichapetalaceae Baill. Dioscoreaceae. Droseraceae Salisb. Ebenaceae Gurke. Elaeacarpaceae Juss. Ericaceae Juss. Eriocaulaceae Martinov. Erythroxylaceae Kunth. Eurphorbiaceae Juss. Fabaceae Lindl. Fagaceae Dumort. Flacourtiaceae Rich. ex DC. Gentianaceae Juss. Geraniaceae Juss. Gesneriaceae Rich. & Juss. Gnetaceae Blume. Gunneraceae Meisn. Haemodoraceae R. Br. Haloragaceae R. Br. Hamamelidaceae R. Br. Heliconiaceae Nakai. Hernandiaceae Blume. Hippocastanaceae A. Rich. Hippocrateaceae Juss. Hugoniaceae Am. Hydrangeaceae Dumort. Through the window, he sees the other children come into the courtyard for ten minutes or so, go back to class. Hydrocharitaceae Juss.

Hydrophyllaceae R. Br. Icacinaceae Miers. Iridaceae Juss. Juglandaceae DC. ex Perleb. Juncaceae Durande. Krameriaceae Dumort. Lacistemataceae Mart. Lamiaceae Martinov. Lauraceae Juss. Lecythidaceae A. Rich. Lemnaceae Martinov. Lennoaceae Solrns. Lentibulariaceae Rich. Lepidobotryaceae J. Léonard. Liliaceae Juss. Limnocharitaceae Takht. ex Cronquist. Linaceae DC. ex Perleb. Loasaceae Juss. Loganiaceae R. Br. ex Mart. Loranthaceae Juss. Lythraceae J. St.-Hil. Magnoliaceae Juss. Malpighiaceae Juss. Malvaceae Juss. Marantaceae R. Br. Marcgraviaceae Bercht. & J. Presl. Maracaceae Kunth. Meliaceae Juss. Mendonciaceae Bremek. Menispermaceae Juss. Menyanthaceae Dumort. Mimosaceae R. Br. Molluginaceae Bartl. Monimiaceae Juss. Monotropaceae Nutt. Moraceae Gaudich. Myricaceae Rich. ex Kunth. Myristicaceae R. Br. Myrsinaceae R. Br. Myrtaceae Juss. Najadaceae Juss. Nyctaginaceae Juss. Nymphaeaceae Sali sb. Ochnaceae DC. Olacaceae R. Br. Oleaceae Hoffmans. & Link. Onagraceae Juss. Opiliaceae Valeton. Orchidaceae Juss. Oxalidaceae R. Br. Papaveraceae Juss. Passifloraceae Juss. ex Roussel. Through the window, he sees the other children come into the courtyard for ten minutes or so, go back to class. Pedaliaceae R. Br. Pellicieraceae L. Beavus. ex. Bullock. Phytolaccaceae R. Br. Pinaceae Spreng. ex Rudolphi, Piperaceae Giseke. Plantaginaceae Juss. Plumbaginaceae Juss. Poaceae Barnhart. Podocarpaceae Endl, Podostemaceae Rich. ex Kunth, Plemoniaceae Juss. Polygalaceae Hoffinans. & Link. Polygonaceae Juss. Pontederiaceae Kunth. Portulacaceae Juss. Potamogetonaceae Bercht. & J. Presl. Primulaceae Batsch ex Borkh. Proteaceae Juss. Pyrolaceae Lindl, Quiinaceae Choisy ex Engl., Rafflesiaceae Dumort. Ranunculaceae Juss. Rhamnaceae Juss. Rhizophoraceae Pers. Rosaceae Juss. Rubiaceae Juss. Ruppiaceae Horan. Rutaceae Juss. Sabiaceae Blume. Salicaceae Mirb. Sapindaceae Juss. Sapotaceae Juss. Scrophulariaceae Juss. Simaroubaceae DC. Smilacaceae Vent. Solanaceae Juss. Styracaceae DC. & Spreng. Surianaceae Am. Symplocaceae Desf. Theaceae Mirb. Theophrastaceae. Thymelaeaceae Juss. Ticodendraceae Gômez-Laur, & L.D. Gômez Tiliaceae Juss. Tovariaceae Pax. Trigoniaceae. Troaeolaceae Juss. ex DC. Turneraceae Kunth ex DC. Typhaceae Juss. Ulmaceae Mirb. Urticaceae Juss. Valerianaceae Batsch. Verbenaceae J. St.-Hil. Violaceae Batsch. Viscaceae Batsch. Vitaceae Juss. Vochysiaceae A. St.-Hil. Winteraceae R. Br. ex Lindl. Xyridaceae C. Agardg. Zamiaceae Horan. Zygophyllaceae

At the end of the day, a woman comes to get him. I'm Béthel. I was with Alejandro when the children found you on the beach. Come, we're going to the cafeteria, brings him to the cafeteria, points to a place for him to sit, next to the other children—Béthel clarifies to him that dinner should take place without chatter. The tot agrees, looks at the other children, who seem like they're used to these instructions. They smile at him—ask him some questions; to understand what happened. The tot eats diligently, discovers tastes he doesn't recognize. He records the information he receives. He is surprised from time to time by the exchanges between the other pupils—which are performed throughout the discrete modification of the table's cartography, a bit of bread, the position of a fork, of a glass of water, hands placed on the table whose fingers, just barely, lift, bend, tilt, the eyes closed sometimes just an instant longer, the manner of carrying foodstuff from the plate to the mouth. They have invented a language, detourning the constraints imposed on them. The kid observes. Tries to understand. Notes the repetitions. Wants to ask them, that they explain it all to him. At the end of the meal, they get up. The kid follows them. Some of them tell him, this same simplified language which they used in the morning, which the adults use, what they're going to do: study, do their homework for tomorrow, then wash up, finally go to bed. Béthel catches up to him in the hall. You don't have to study tonight. I'm going to show you where you're going to take a shower. The other children watch him walk away with Béthel. They make it to the dormitory, Béthel shows him his bed, beside, his nightstand, inside, a towel, a bar of soap. Come, it's this way. The kid stops. Waits for her to notice. Turns toward him. Why am I not staying with the other children? Why can't I be with them? It's not that you can't, she emphasizes this gesture, it's that today you should learn how the orphanage is set up. The others have to do what they do every day. Your arrival mustn't change what they do every day, you understand? The kid shrugs his shoulders, walks toward her, all right. Tomorrow you'll go to class with them, and you'll be able to spend time with them. All right. So I'll show you the showers. It's this way, come. The kid follows her. She shows him how everything works. I'll wait for you in the dormitory, come when you're done. The kid washes himself thoroughly—as he has learned to, as the huntress-gatheress taught him to. He sighs. He dries off just as thoroughly. He meets Béthel. Feeling better? It was very nice, thanks. Would you like to tell me your story? I told it to Bitsie this morning. I wasn't there, would you like to tell it to me? Bitsie and Randy haven't told you it? They did. Yes, they told me what you explained to them; but I would like to hear it from you. Why? Just because, because I would like that. They don't believe me, you don't believe me, why should I tell you something that you're not going to believe and that you already know? I want to leave here; it was really nice to want to take care of me, to look out for me and give me food, but I want to go be with the huntress-gatheress. The huntress-gatheress? The one I came here with; I see in your eyes that you don't believe me; I can also see that you want to know if I'm going to say something different from what I told Bitsie this morning, it's pointless; I want to leave and I'm going to leave; what I don't get is why you think I have to stay here; I know how to hunt, I know how to keep an eye out, I know I can find her if I leave tomorrow. We can't let you leave like that, it's not possible, we must take care of you, you're too young to make it by yourself; if you leave, you're going to find the city, and you're going to steal, or get picked up by one of the gangs, you won't have anyone to protect you. The huntress-gatheress protected me, I protected her. The kid's gestures are fast, cutting, nervous. Until we found you. Your story is different from the ones the other children tell us when they arrive here, but everyone wants to leave the orphanage—in the beginning, every child wants to go back, in this your story is the same, you understand? I didn't make this story up. But you want to leave? Yes. You will have to wait until you are older, when you're older you'll be able to choose to stay, or leave—even I, you see, I chose to stay, and when I arrived here, I wanted to leave—like you. You grew up here? Yes. You know how to speak like the other children? Yes. Not like Randy? No, Randy came here when he was already grown up. Can you teach me? Yes; if you decide to stay. The kid shrugs his shoulders. Béthel says, make gestures he doesn't understand anymore. I was saying: I will teach you if you stay. Can you repeat those gestures? She starts again. The gestures, according to what he knows, are cut short, faster. And others are added, very brief, which don't involve the hands. These children's eyes at the table, their longer blinking, hardly longer, which the kid had observed. The other children come back from study. They watch the kid who is with Béthel, don't come see him, gather their things, go wash up. Béthel gets up, explains I should supervise, to make sure everything goes well. The kid watches the children, finds them calm. She follows his eyes, adds they are calm because someone is supervising them, otherwise it would be—the kid doesn't understand the gesture, doesn't ask for it to be repeated, is tired. Tired of being supervised. He lies down on his bed while Béthel closes the blinds, turns on the lamps, busy—late, then posts up at one end of the dormitory. The coming and going of the children to the shower is restful. Certain ones take books and read while waiting for a place to open up. Two by two, certain others converse. Occasionally he looks at Béthel sitting still, almost absent. When all the children have come back, she lets a moment pass for everyone to get into bed, and, in the interim, certain ones are still chatting in pairs— those ones watch the clock regularly, and from time to time look at the kid who is trying to understand what they are telling each other, and why nobody is approaching him, nor him them—even though this morning, in the courtyard, they surrounded him, asked him questions, wanted to know, were talkative. Béthel makes a sign to say she is going to turn off the light, asks them to get into bed, to set something up around their bed, walks between the beds to make sure everyone is indeed in bed, under the covers, she walks alongside certain ones, occasionally tidies the folds of the—mosquito nets, wishes them a good night, turns off the light and leaves. A few moments in the black. His eyes get used to the half-darkness— the light behind the blinds. The kid looks at the mosquito net that envelops his bed, beyond, the ceiling. He listens. Some of the children are already sleeping, others fidgeting, almost silently. He waits. He waits for silence. The way the huntress-gatheress would fall asleep so quickly, this memory shakes him. He gets up, walks to the window, open, with closed blinds. Lifts, pulls the handle of the catch toward him, parts the blinds. Looks down below, the blacks of the forest and the sea, the city, its lights. He slept for two days. The day is coming to an end. It will be three days that he's been separated from the huntress-gatheress. Three days. There may still be traces of their arrival on the shore. But it's already cold. She must have already left—in search of him. In the city? He will have to leave tomorrow. Tomorrow morning, he will have to leave the orphanage. Someone's coming, he hears their footsteps on the floor, he waits. A boy his age leans his elbow on the window, such that his hands are visible. You can't stay there. If they find you at the window, if they see that you opened the blinds, you're going to get in trouble. You have to go back to bed. Before someone comes. Why? That's just how it is. They don't let us. They don't let us talk when the lights are out. You're going to tell them? What? Are you going to tell them I got up? The boy stares at him. He articulates, without a sound, exaggerating it, loco. Loco! He taps his temple at the same time with his index finger. The kid extends his hand to him. The boy shakes it. They look at each other. The boy continues now you have to go back to bed, I'm going to close the blinds, I'm used to it, it will make less noise, we'll talk tomorrow. The kid agrees. He may be gone tomorrow, but he likes the boy—would the huntress-gatheress like him? The kid turns around, is held back by the arm. The other says my name's Digmar. And you? Tomorrow, an evasive gesture. Tomorrow? The tot smiles to him, steals away to his bed, slips under the mosquito net. The blinds are closed—gently, without a sound, as Digmar had assured him. The tot looks at the mosquito net. Tomorrow. Why not tomorrow. Tomorrow in the thread of the mosquito net. Tomorrow. Tomorrow on the roof. Tomorrow, he pulls his blankets up to be covered. Digmar. The huntress-gatheress. The baby dead. Dzeta dead. The huntress-gatheress' face. Tomorrow. It's early. The kid crosses the courtyard—the children are playing there, leaving the cafeteria, where they just had their breakfast. Digmar catches up to him. Where are you going? I'm leaving. I have to find her. But you can't leave. The watchman; the watchman won't let you out. I want to leave. I want to find her. I have to get out of here. The kid makes his way, determined, toward the main hall. Digmar catches up with him again. He accompanies him, without trying to stop him. Together they go into the building, come back out. Digmar stops, watches the kid advancing toward the exit. The gatehouse of the watchman. Who comes out, stops the kid, leads him back toward the hall, holding him by the arm, elbow up. The watchman and the kid are a sight for Digmar—the kid calm, the watchman angry. I'm taking him to Bitsie—and I'm going to tell her that you were with him. Go to class right now. The kid makes a soothing gesture to Digmar—don't worry. From the hall, Digmar heads for the courtyard; the watchman and the kid toward the office of the supervisors. They enter. Only Bitsie is there. The watchman explains the situation succinctly to her. Bitsie thanks him. Makes a sign for him to return to the entrance. The watchman goes out, closes the door. The kid faces Bitsie. You have to let me leave. We can't—Béthel already explained this to you. She, she was taking care of me. Then she will come to find you here—her gestures are interrupted, cut off by the brutality of the kid's; she is as real as me and just as alive! Then, she will come to find you here, there's no doubt about it. How will she know I'm here?

She will go looking in the city, and someone will tell her about the orphanage, there's no doubt, everyone in Managua knows the orphanage. Now you should go to class. I'm going to come with you. I want to go look for her instead. If I wait too long, the traces will be wiped away, they might already be. Look, for now, you are going to go to class. Then we'll see. Bitsie gets up. Come. The kid hesitates for a second then obeys, follows her. They cross back through the courtyard. Arrive at a classroom. Bitsie makes a sign through the window, they go in. She shows him a place in the back of the room, asks him to go sit there, meets with the teacher, quickly explains the situation to her. The children watch the kid, the two adults. Everyone knows where he was found. The kid recognizes Digmar, and a few other faces he had seen the night before, in the morning. He smiles. Bitsie gives him a look, then seeing him smiling, smiles as well, relieved. She leaves. Class resumes, the teacher makes a sign to one of the students to give some paper and a pencil to the tot, interrupts her gesture then asks him his name. He gives the same answer as he gave to Digmar, the night before. Tomorrow. Your name is Tomorrow? Yes. She raises an eyebrow, suspicious, pauses for a second, then repeats, Tomorrow. Welcome. We are going to resume our class. Try to follow along, I'll come see you after; the history of Nicaragua is the subject. Pointing to the chalkboard, a title, she resumes her monologue where she had left off. The tot observes the other children, they write in their notebooks, are occasionally asked a question. So he begins writing, listening only to be able, in case he were asked a question, to give an answer, resuming the explanation which had just been given. He writes. Rather than a map of the orphanage, legible to everyone, notes, his written language is foreign here, what he has seen, tries to find the solution for how to get out—escape. Decides to find whomever found him and convince him, her, them to bring him to this place. Watches Digmar, concentrated. Every pupil is. Resumes: the garden in the back, the dormitory window overlooking the park which leads to the city, someone coming if there is any noise in the dormitory, the study he has not yet seen, the showers, the least monitored place, maybe the moment of his shower, not to come back, the one keeping watch will notice immediately, he was found during a field trip, do they happen often? He'll have to ask the children—Digmar. Class ends. The teacher comes to see him while the other children are leaving—he's going to miss his chance to talk to them. And how was it? She walks behind him, looks over his shoulder at the notes he took—cannot read them, aren't in Spanish, but inspects them for a time. You don't speak our language? Actually, I do, this one—and his hands move, without saying anything. But not Spanish? No, not Spanish, but I can learn. The teacher smiles, goes to her desk, organizes her things, erases the chalkboard, the tot stays still, sitting, a teacher enters, the teacher leaves, the second class begins. The kid resumes—the door in the front is guarded, the watchman can't be bribed, and the children are afraid of him—Digmar was acting scared of him this morning, even though he came along. After the second break, he is allowed to leave. In the courtyard, Randy and Béthel who come to speak with him kindly, how's it going?, it's not too hard?, preventing him from talking to the other children. The next class is a hands-on class—in the farm I showed you yesterday, they are in the middle of leaving. Randy points in the same direction they had taken, and the line of children heads that way—two by two. The tot joins it, alone, last. Once out of the building, a child is there next to him, then he is moved to the front, the children sliding along without breaking the rhythm of their steps, nor breaking the appearance of successive rows of two. He finds himself next to Digmar—only his left hand, between the two of them, moves, hardly, asks him how's it going? He says fine, with his head, one time. His hand again, but it's moving too fast, the gestures are too brief for the tot to grasp—when would the ones he can understand become visible. He replies as best he can, piecing together something like possible talk? Digmar answers him, the kid understands, soon. They keep walking, out to the farm. There, the class sets off again in a group—every pupil knows what to do. Each group accomplishing specific tasks, the teacher is less severe, busier—notices nothing when Digmar pulls the kid away—they go to look for straw in the barn. Digmar explains they're afraid of the language we speak, they don't understand it, except for Béthel, but she's nice, even if she grew up here and wants to protect this place, she understands a little better than the others why we speak differently to each other. They're afraid? Yes. Why? Because they can't know exactly what's going on between us I imagine; maybe they're afraid we'll leave. What would happen if you left?, I don't understand, you're . . . I feel like you'd all be capable of fending for yourselves, wouldn't you? Maybe yes, not all of us, that's for sure, it depends. Do you like living here? It's not worse than anywhere else, we learn a lot of stuff. But you can't leave when you want, when can you get out of here? When we're grown up. Grown up? Older than 16, or when we seem like we're ready, they're the ones who choose, who find us a place to go—to work. I don't want to stay here, I want to find the huntress-gatheress, I have to get out of here, do you know a way? Too late, we have to go back with the straw, otherwise she'll notice you came with me, we'll get yelled at if she notices. The kid remains dumbfounded—that Digmar brought him here to tell him that, almost like the others, like the people in charge. But: later. And: learn from them. But: her. He follows him, no longer knowing what he should do, how to get him to say more—about the way to get out, the kid feels like he knows, feels like he knows something else too, feels Digmar's curiosity for him. To wait like the huntress-gatheress taught him, wait for the right moment, don't be contrary, find the loophole, without being stubborn, with the territory, wait until t,he,y are convinced.

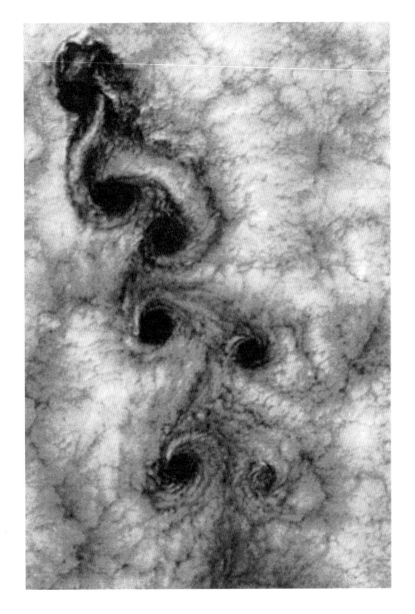

This is where you were. The kid walks around the area. Up to the edge of the bayou. They see a tree, around which seashell necklaces lie fraying. The kid finds the path and they climb back up it. At the end, traces of ancient, disappearing dwellings. The forest is taking over the main square. I want to find her. Odili explodes YOU HAVE TO TELL HIM. Digmar and Adriana look at her, vaguely, undecided, she continues. We found her too. Before you. We just passed the place we found her a second ago. She was lying closer to the forest. She was sleeping. She was alone. Her breath was steady. It's not really a beach where people come to swim. But it was an adult, we've learned not to get mixed up in the lives of adults. We kept walking. We found you. In a raft. With a dead baby next to you. You were really shaky. You were making these movements with your arms, your hands. We understood: dead! You were talking a little like us, you were abandoned, you were all abandoned, a baby was dead. We decided to carry you to Alejandro and Béthel. Passing by her again, some of us were saying you'd arrived together. We looked at her. We looked at you. You don't look like each other. So the girls and boys who were carrying you kept on walking. You weren't doing well. The older kids said we'd have to move fast. The girls and boys who weren't carrying you, the younger ones, made her a shelter with two sticks and some fabric. She woke up that very moment, she started to talk. Nobody understood. She wasn't from here. A foreigner could have wanted to come swim here, alone. We didn't know. She started wanting to articulate a movement. Some of the kids said it wasn't anything. Not a word. Just a movement. She was weak. Nobody knew what to think of her. Digmar came back to find us. He had been running, he was out of breath, they had decided to take you right away. We had to leave her—right away, get back to the minibus. We tried to explain what had just happened. We started moving. Nobody would listen to us. Then—because of the dead baby in the raft, because you were making gestures like ours, because you were like us, abandoned, as nobody was listening to us, we decided to keep quiet. Not to talk about her. To say we'd found you all alone on the beach. Odili adds that's how it all happened. The kid's steely face repeats I want to find her. I don't know how I'm going to do it but I'm going to find her. Why?, why don't you stay with us?, we're the same. Why wouldn't you stay with us? She didn't abandon me. Adriana makes a gesture which the kid doesn't understand. Digmar says no. What? What does that mean, huh? We're not allowed to talk about it. About what? Adriana makes the gesture again it means we're not allowed to talk about it. Taboo. What's taboo? The question I want to ask you. What question? Adriana consults the other two children with her eyes, sighs, is your mother the one who's looking for you? Digmar bats at the air with his hand, looking displeased. What's it matter? She didn't abandon me; I want to find her. And the dead baby? It's not her fault. It just happened. Where are you all going? On the 20, Odili, Digmar, and Adriana don't understand, the place that's drawn on the 20, still not understood. The kid explains the Chinese money. Odili asks do you think she's looking for you, do you, or that she's already left to go there? The kid continues, without answering Odili, do you know anyone who could have lived here? They're always moving around, it's not easy to find them. Do you know someone I can ask? They go quiet. Odili says yes, maybe in the city, I know who to ask. Immediately Adriana adds we can't go there now, we have to go back to the orphanage, otherwise... Otherwise what? Odili asks. We're going to have to leave the orphanage one time or another, we're going to grow up. I'd rather do it now, instead of being placed somewhere, with no choice. I'd rather leave now. I don't want to end up like Béthel. And then. Also it's out fault that they were separated. Odili says to the kid if you're ok with it I'll leave with you, I'll go look for her with you. Digmar and Adriana look at each other, look at the kid and Odili.

Assis en haut,

at the threshold,
her strength is the heart, its output,
its sweetness and fury, heard,
every escarpment, every
observed change in season
all in knots and carried away,

son amour qui chasse et cueille   cervidae
revient   oiseaux
et attend   poissons
et retourne à la chasse   animaux
         langues, c,us,toms, knowledge
         pour cueillir   baies
             souvenirs tissés   champignons
                 leurs   légumes
           lointains   fruits
         dans un pays où ensemble
             regardaient
             toutes
               les conséquences historiques   d'
             1
             1   somme   de
                                   choix
             1   nourri
                                     it
   dos
    à   c
  dosffffffffffa   e,s
               d
et du vent   souffle
et du flou   monte du fleuve
                   tissé autour des pics karstiques
   love   sifflotant u n   vieil   air
         au derrière
            de la frontière
   dos
    dos   sifflements font phrases   je vois
                 a   humming-bird
                          humming-bird
revient   je n'ai pas de   flèches
viens   —tu as attendu assez   maintenant
maintenant

104

From the freight ship she boarded, the huntress-gatheress watches the coast recede. In no hospital in Managua could she find the kid. In the city, no trace of him Disappeared. She left ● traces of herself all over, and everywhere she left ● ● ● messages for the tot. Everywhere she said where she was going, everywhere she showed the 20 yuan bill. If he's alive, he'll meet me there, way out where we were going together.

NOTEBOOK

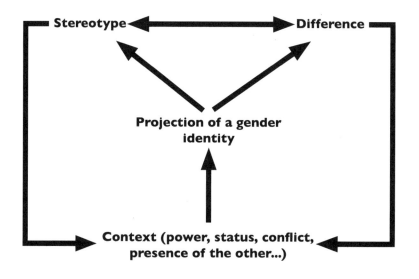

When psychology compares
men and women
:
from science to stereotypes
&
vice
versa

Olivier Klein, Researcher/Lecturer
Department of Social Psychology, Vrije Universiteit Brussel
E-mail: oklein@ulb.ac.be

* *

Secondly, the looks of each human being were as a whole round, with back and sides in a circle. And each had four arms, and legs equal in number to his arms, and two faces alike in all respects on a cylindrical neck, but there was one head for both faces – they were set in opposite directions – and four ears, and two sets of genitals [...]. The races of human beings were three, not two as now, male and female; for there was also a third race that shared in both, a race whose name still remains, though it itself has vanished. For at that time one race was androgynous, and in looks and name it combined both, the male as well as the female; but now it does not exist except for the name that is reserved for reproach. [...] Each used to walk upright too, just as one does now, in whatever direction he wanted; and whenever he had the impulse to run fast, then just as tumblers with their legs straight out actually move around as they tumble in a circle, so did they, with their eight limbs as supports, quickly move in a circle. [...] Now, they were awesome in their strength and robustness, and they had great and proud thoughts, so they made an attempt on the gods.[1]

* *

1 - Plato. *Plato's "Symposium"*. Translated by Seth Benardete, The University of Chicago Press, 2001.

She had done something of which her father disapproved, but no one could recall what. Even so, her father had dragged her to the cliff and hurled her into the sea. The fish had eaten her flesh, devoured her eyes. And she lay motionless in the water, her skeleton tossing in the current. One day a fisherman arrived. In fact, more than one had come to fish these waters, but this one in particular had been pulled quite far from his home and he did not know that the local fishermen kept their distance from this creek, claiming it was haunted. When all of a sudden the the fisherman's hook became snared in the ribcage of the Skeleton Woman. "Oh," the fisherman thought, "I've got a big catch!" He was already imagining the number of people this magnificent fish was going to feed, how long it would last, how long a break it would give him from fishing. Then, while he was battling this enormous weight, the sea began to boil, shaking his kayak like a wisp of straw, for the woman below the surface was struggling to free herself. And the more she fought, the more entangled she became in the line. Try as she might, she was pulled inexorably upward, hooked by the ribs. The hunter turned to gather his net. He did not see then her bald skull appear above the waves. Nor did he see the small coral creatures which sparkled around her, nor yet the crustaceans upon her old ivory teeth. When he turned with his net, the entire body had emerged and hung at the far end of his kayak by her long front teeth. "Aaah!" the man howled. Out of terror, his heart gave a terrible leap and his eyes went to take refuge in the back of his head, as his ears turned crimson. "Aaah!" He dealt her a blow with the paddle and started rowing like a madman for the shore. He hadn't realized she was still wrapped up in his line. And so she seemed to be chasing him, standing up on her feet. He was more and more terrified. Zig-zag as he might, she followed, and her breath gave off vaporous clouds above the water, and her arms strained outward, as if to seize him and drag him into the depths. "Aaaaaaah!" he moaned, touching dry land. He took not a single leap from his kayak and already he was running, clutching his fishing rod, with its line, the Skeleton Woman's white coral corpse behind him, completely entangled. He climbed the boulders. She followed. He set off over the frozen plain. She followed. He ran over the fish someone had set out to dry, reducing them to pieces under his mukluks. She followed all the while. In truth, she grabbed a bit of dried fish in passing and started to eat it, for it had been quite a while since she last ate. At last, the man made it to his igloo, dove into the tunnel, and crawled back to its center on all fours. Out of breath, he waited there, hiccuping in the darkness, his heart beating furiously. Safe at last, oh yes, yes, by the gods' grace, Crow, yes, thank you, Crow, and Sedna the all-nurturing, safe at last . . . When suddenly, as he lit his whale oil lamp, there it was, she was there, hunched on the snowy ground, a heel over her shoulder, a knee against her rib cage, a foot upon her elbow. Later on, he would be unable to say what pushed him—perhaps the fire's glow softened her features, or it may well have been that he was a lonely man. Whatever the case, the fisherman's breath grew more attentive, then, gently, he reached out his tough hands and, with the words of a mother to her child, began disentangling her from the fishing line. "Na, na . . ." He started by disentangling the line from her toes, then from her heels. "Na, na . . ." He worked until nightfall, whereupon he clothed her in furs to keep her warm. And the Skeleton Woman's bones were in the proper order. He searched in his leather garments, took his flint and made use of a few pieces of his hair as a fire starter. As he oiled the precious wood of his fishing rod, and reeled in its line, he watched her. She, in his furs, said nothing—she didn't dare—for fear he would take hold of her, throw her against the rocks and break her into pieces. The man began to doze off. He slipped under the skins and soon began to dream. And yet at times, in the slumber of humans, a tear pearls upon their eyelid; we don't know what type of dream is the cause, but these must be sad dreams, or indeed dreams expressive of desire. This is what happened with the man. The Skeleton Woman saw his tear glisten in the firelight and suddenly, she was terribly thirsty. She unfolded her bones and slid over to the sleeping man, pressed her mouth to the tear. This lone tear was like a river to her parched lips. She drank again and again, until slaking the thirst which had burned within her for so long. While she lay beside him, she plunged her hand into the sleeping man and refreshed his heart, that powerful drum. She sat and knocked on the two sides of his heart: "Boom, boom! Boom, boom!" As she played like this, she began humming: "Flesh, flesh, flesh!" And the more she sang, the more her body was covered with flesh. She sang for a head of hair, she sang for eyes, she sang for plump hands. She sang for a cleft between her legs, for breasts long and deep enough to keep warm, and everything a woman needs. And when this was finished, she sang for the removal of the sleeping man's clothes and slid into bed with him, skin against skin. She returned to his body the magnificent drum of his heart, and that is how they awoke, each raveled differently in the other, now, after the previous night, in good and lasting fashion. The people who have forgotten the cause of her woe, in the beginning, tell that she went off with the fisherman and that they were amply fed by the sea creatures she had known during her time underwater. This story, they say, is true, and they have nothing to add.

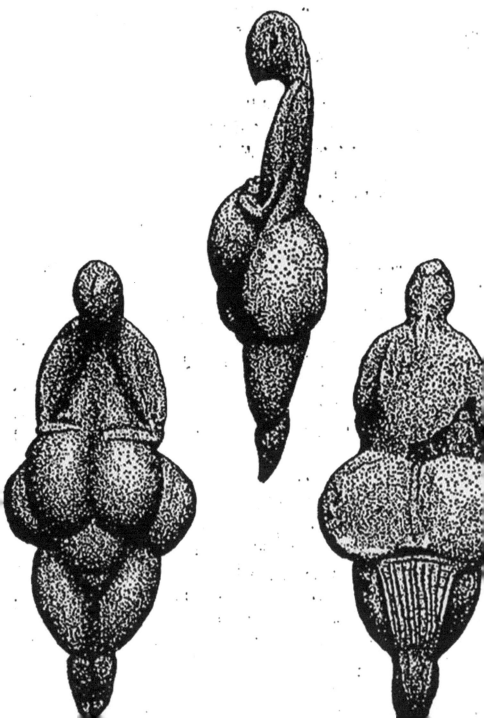

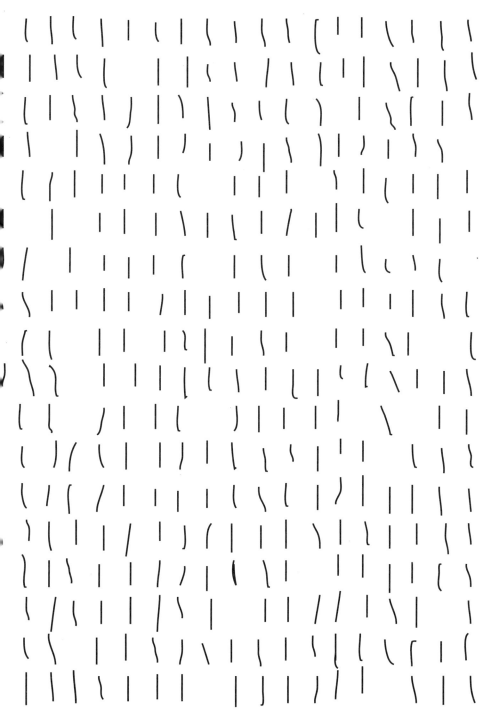

THE NAME AND THE FORM[1]

Nâgasena, you have spoken
of Name-and-Form.
But what is Name and what is Form?

What is material, is Form;
states intellectual and sensual,
are Name.

Why cannot Name be born again in isolation,
or Form in isolation?

For they rely the one upon the other,
and always together they are born.

The hen, for example; were there in her no seed,
no egg would take form:
the seed and the egg are conditioned, the one by the other;
their birth is simultaneous.
Likewise, were there no Name,
there would be no Form;
Name and Form are conditioned, the one by the other;
their birth is simultaneous.
And so are they produced
over
an indefinite
period of time.

---

1 - *Les questions de Milinda (Milinda-Pañha)* [*The Questions of Milinda*], French trans. Louis Finot, Bossard, 1923. Book II, 24.
Le Nom et la Forme [The Name and the Form], p. 92. Available at: http://www.lesquestionsdemilinda.org/les_questions_de_milinda/livre_2.htm#chap_24

Such imprecision is fairly common in
[that] which isn't subject to strict rules; it's
[that] which makes the law

and

no authority can decide

Okay, there. There we are. At the foot of the wall. To know if it will hold;
if we will make it hold, if we'll reinforce it (leaves, branches, dirt, scree, and
little stones: all the materials of the dams we're going to find a way around it, if
we're going to climb it, if we're going to build over the rivers' course might),
destroy it. There we are. Sun, wind, water. At the foot of work at the foot of the if, of

Such imprecisions are fairly common in
[that] which is drawn, decides, dances, describes, scream p l e t e w e s [that] which returns in memory
[that] which listens,

which

and which

the vocabulary of
the usage

the proper language
proper usage of language

[that] which won't: don't
[that] which does not do; [dunno]
[that] which will do, won't

[that] which
[that] which hold;
if

the if of the
if
h

artery little story, an improvised story on

it's inside—it has several forms—so it doesn't get out; it got out, it's

I understood something

yes,

something:

a humming-bird flying around the
scarlet red of un unknown flower, whose
stem crawls and wraps around, up a
vertical and metallic rod, which
holds up a sheetmetal roof and
initiates a barrier, keeping it from
falling toward a river's cove
dominated by this ledge which faces the
surging, rocky peaks turbanned with mist

ignacy

一 这儿
二

20

Océan
glacial Arctique

Pôle
Nord

the growing distance, this absurdity
absurde comme une clé qui ouvre des frontières
de nulle part, la terre de laquelle je viens

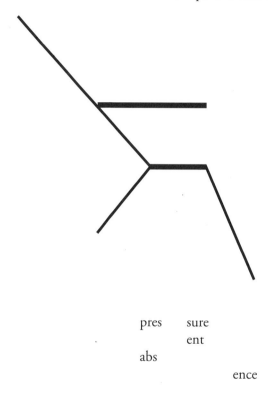

pres   sure
       ent
abs

        ence

(scent)
present absent pressure = pressing-*sentence*

COURAGE !

when the punctum is too obvious (red) well it isn't because we don't look at it anymore because it's in someone else's memory that it

3.94 in

* *

The most complete prehistoric skeletons, as much as the contour of human parietal bones up to this day, demonstrate no marked difference in height or strength between the two sexes, and more than one researcher has recognized that it is ostensibly the division of tasks according to sex which has brought about, and very slowly at that, this difference which today can be observed everywhere.[1]

* *

separates

from the human body
gender from form

the distance
by which

separate   separate obese   deadnizens

dead   emaciated   like   is an   are separated

is an   disgendered

disgendered extreme   extreme

disgendered extreme

* *

*The world presents us
with a huge amount
of information, so
we*

often take shortcuts to help process it all (this is known as the 'cognitive miser'), Carothers explained to Raw Story in an email. One of those shortcuts is a tendency to categorize things - it's easier to think of 2 things (men are one way and women are another) than to think of all of the nuances of overlapping distributions, particularly if they're not brought to our attention when we hear about an average difference.

* *

1 - Françoise d'Eaubonne, *Les femmes avant le patriarcat* [*Women before the Patriarchy*], Payot, 1976, p. 32.

Until 1906, when education adopted the thesis of the oocyte's fertilization by a single spermatazoon and the collaboration of the two sexes in reproduction, and the Faculté de Paris announced this truth ex cathedra, the doctors were still divided into two camps; those who believed, like Claude Bernard, that women alone possessed the principle of life, like our ancestors in pre-patriarchal societies (the ovist theory); and those who imagined, in the manner of certain current indigenous tribes cited by W. Lederer, that the male ejaculated a minuscule homunculus, perfectly formed, which the female belly received, nourished, and developed in the same way humus allows a seed to grow.[1&2]

* *

We are pregnant.
prégnant we, are
pregnant.

* *

Elles pourtant ont chassé ensemble.
Presque jusqu'à la parturition.
Pendant la grossesse.

---

1 - Françoise d'Eaubonne, *Les femmes avant le patriarcat* [*Women before the Patriarchy*], op. cit., p. 11.
2 - A theory was posed according to which the women, no longer hunting (whatever the reasons may have been—the most commonly given being childbirth, for which the woman was visibly responsible, and which found a possible reflection in the figure of the great goddess) became, by observation, the inventors hoe-driven agriculture—and this hypothesis could also be extended to those women and men whose bodies were no longer fit for the hunt, whether their bodies were wounded, malformed, or too old.

It seems that women have made few contributions to the discoveries and inventions in the history of civilization; there is, however, one technique which they may have invented—that of plaiting and weaving. If that is so, we should be tempted to guess the unconscious motive for the achievement. Nature herself would seem to have given the model which this achievement imitates by causing the growth at maturity of the pubic hair that conceals the genitals. The step that remained to be taken lay in making the threads adhere to one another, while on the body they stick into the skin and are only matted together. If you reject this idea as fantastic and regard my belief in the influence of the lack of a penis on the configuration of femininity as an idée fixe, I am of course defenceless.[2]

* *

—*Peut-on dire   ?*
    "Nous sommes enceints"
—Ce n'est pas commun, mais ça se dit, oui.

* *

```
                                    how to
                                  oneself
                                    again
                                       ?
```

---

1 - As with agriculture, the men and women who no longer hunted, half-sedentary, are supposed to have invented pottery. This invention would complete that of agriculture, allowing for the conservation of seeds and harvests. This invention, linked to water (the amniotic sac, the menstrual cycle, the moon) and to the earth (the Great Goddess, the Earth Mother, the responsibility of women in childbirth, and, its mirror, in burial, allowing for the rebirth of the person to whom this homage is paid) is generally associated with the feminine.

2 - Freud, S. (1933). *New Introductory Lectures on Psychoanalysis.* Lecture 33: "Femininity." Standard Edition, v. 22. pp. 136-157.

deified, warriors

divinisée, grand-déesse

anthropo morphism &   animisms

mechanisms

* *

ASIDE FROM ∫*orm* ∫*ormless** **ungender**
deified (f.)

* *

[…] Venus of Lespugue […]
[…] Venus of Willendorf […]
gravid breasts bellies ass thighs

* *

* *

What a big [throat] *you have!* [2]

* *

---

1 - Lecureux and Cheret, Rahan. Vol. 33 : *Les rivages interdits* [*The Forbidden Shores*], Paris, Vaillant, 1978, p. 29.
2 - Rabelais, *Gargantua*, Le livre de Poche, 1972, p. 85.
Like the great eaters, runners, fighters, like the sweetly halfwitted and big-hearted, likewise leading an errant life, Gargantua is a mirror of Gargan, himself the son of the goddess Belisama, the "all-brilliant or all-radiant" goddess of domesticated fire, of the metallurgic arts (particularly that associated with the weapon forge) and the art of braiding, who, though she remained virgin, is supposed to have been fertilized by the divine spirit of the god Belenos.

GRADATIONS & INTERCONNECTIONS

GRADATIONS & INTERCONNECTIONS

GRADATIONS & INTERCONNECTIONS

GRADATIONS & INTERCONNECTIONS

GRADATIONS & INTERCONNECTIONS

* *

ASIDE FROM *form formless* **ungender**
warrior

* *

in   every   culture,   tradition—myth,   legend,
whether   it   deals   with   divinities   or
queens—has   the   huntress   be   a   virgin.[1]

* *

would be shapeless from power
the bodies resuming their shape
the power in a shape, multiple
the power-hunting
the power-birthing
&

* *
* *

[...] Venus of Tursac [...]
[...] Lady of Sireuil [...]
[...]

---

1 - Françoise d'Eaubonne, *Les femmes avant le patriarcat* [*Women before the Patriarchy*], op. cit., p. 57.
2 - *The Lady of Sireuil* (Calcite, 9.2cm, Sireuil, France) unites the pregnant form, its belly and ass, and the phallic, its breasts, glans, its torso, two cavernous bodies, its ass, a pair of balls..

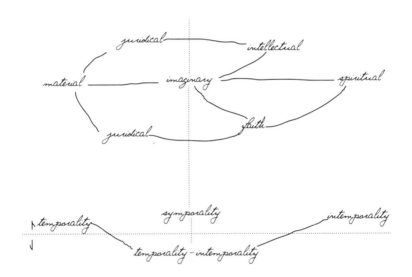

ΙΓΠΟΥΤΗ

ΔΕΙΝΟΜΑΤΗ

Of precision, aesthetics tends to think in terms of the clear-cut, a straight line cutting through, separative, constitutive of edges. What lips part slightly to let out which humors, which scents, which breaths, which words bearing what consequences? What blade of which tool makes the incision that allows for an erotic precision to emerge from aesthetics? Whether of the seamstress, in the 12th century, or of Atropos, in antiquity, scissors open at the axle of their visible head, often rounded and protruding, sometimes cleft, sometimes screw-shaped, sometimes positioned higher than whatever it is that is sealed; such a penile clitoris or vagina full from end to end, they retain the leg-blades which could, like a feminist drawing from the seventies, sever the head of this mantis' lover, cut off life, and of the crime leave only its weapon hanging benignly from the belt, on and between the folds of a long skirt, or stashed away in a sewing basket, where the scissors sit beside a number of other accessories, certain of which, such as the thimble, bring sex toys to mind. Passage from the plural to the singular, from the feminine attribute to the masculine, the chisel—or ciseau in French, whose plural, ciseaux, means scissors— "represent the cosmic and active (male) principle which penetrates and modifies the passive (female) principle. […] But even as an agent, they are acted upon. They are active in relation to matter, but passive in relation to the mallet or the hand, which themselves represent the Will in action." Straight razors, switchblades are kept closed, pocketed beside a flaccid member, where the correlation with an erection materializes as a hand removes it from a first sheath, exposes and opens it, unfolded to double its length, beyond foreskin, a great distance to the hinge, the blade. A machete allows you to enter deep into the moist danger of a virgin forest; the ax chops it down to its trunks, the sap oozes, under the hard skin the blond sweetness of concentric rings is revealed. The elegant sword and dagger, the brutal cutlass and poignard, parting the lips of the wound. Of the knife, the most everyday use takes place in the kitchen where, in Japan, for example, cutting is a precise art which requires, it is said, seven years of study. In modern art, Lucio Fontana's razor, in 1959, made an incision in the surface of a canvas stretched on a frame;

into the slit he created passed, from The Origin of the World, *93 years. A razor which could have, in a tragic love story, opened the length of a v(e/a)in, or, in seduction, slid over the surface of the skin to let it appear, to let appear, quivering with a Saloméan eroticism, the life of a carotid. Louis XVI, a fetishist of locks, helped Doctor Guillotin to develop, paving the way for his own death, the cleanest and most clinical, most precise, most humane death, the blade to beat all blades, which would later enable Danton to tell his executioner: "Show my head to the people, it is worth seeing." That the perfection of a blade be associated with the French Revolution, the Reign of Terror, comes as no surprise. "From that point on," said Philippe Sollers, "everything gets called into question, notably the questions we might term erotic or sexual. That is why, once you look into this major event, it becomes clear to what extent its most profound implications have been suppressed." Scissors, feminine in the collective imagination, perhaps because of their association with one of the Parcae, assume from the outset a form capable of embracing the amplitude of legs, arms, blades. The latter, sliding from one exterior to another, create new edges and an equal number of excenters. If they stab something in a carried-away, violent gesture, it will be the heart, an eye, live tissue that holds them inside, the blades of scissors never being turned toward the exterior of the interior—unlike other blades. And after the plunging-in comes the pulling-out, the parting of these blades, then a repenetration by only one of these two, finally the cut, a slide-slice, from the center toward the exterior. Slicing cleanly, they ensure the penetration of a uniform surface, of a penetrated surface, an unerect member, the permanence of its opening: a mouth, a sex, an anus. So these blades, phallic for the most part, allow us, beyond doing away with the masculine, not to remain in the ungendered, the neuter, but to create the feminine— such as in the creation of its ultimate accomplishment, Aphrodite, once the gonads of her father, sliced by time, mixed with the foam, the indistinct, the imprecise, the formless, the sea opens to let its goddess appear out of love and pleasure. To designate the depth of an entity:*

its hidden complexity, to make two out of one, to designate a passage, from life to death, from flesh to art, the desire for precision is foremost a desire for spreading apart and making appear, for dispersal and separation, almost for opposition (when the will cannot come before understanding, judgement in opposition to the masculine and feminine), to the point of Manichaeism. From right to wrong, like a grammar handbook? Maurice Grévisse's, in mind, on hand, helps one enjoy the most correct expression, satisfy the respect of formally decreed rules. Pushed to absurdity, there is a movement from -ise to -ious, from precise to precious. Banning even the supposedly vulgar, Preciosity avoids all sounds that so much as hint at it, even if it means they are destined (impossible word) to become(oh!) affected. If Molière mocked, in his The Precious Young Ladies, under the name of Magdelon, the movement's most famous and as(mon dieu!) tute instigator, Madeleine de Scudéry, we owe to this woman the still-current Map of Tendre. Giving herself the last name of Sappho, sometimes signing her novels with her brother's name, Georges, De Scudéry was opposed to marriage, rightfully judged it as violent when imposed, and indeed never signed any marriage cunt(ah!)ract. In this sense Madeleine de Scudéry was a feminist, and Preciosity widely contributed to the rejection of mas(help!)culine superiority as a given. Working at the level of language, thanks to its intuitive -prehension of language's influence on thought, certainly the opposite of today, where the tendency would be to add suffixes, its contribution was, among others, to sever certain heads, those of words, certain prefixes, so the gender-related not blossom from one's mouth, remaining a young girl, never amputated from her patronym (certainly still the pater's, but so long ago, etc.), never replaced by another man's. Preciosity, with its extreme assiduity, avoiding the territory of the lascivious at all costs, rivals, with its arabesques, its workarounds: its neologisms, its hyperboles, its witty pricks and metaphors, the language for which the Baroque opts, and ultimately rejoins it. If the sources of their desires are, a priori, opposite, none cedes the territory of

formal inventiveness, nor that of love. Established by women,
Preciosity only wants to see in love its feeling, this Map of Tendre,
their witty remarks (such innocence!) at every moment appeal to the
wit, reflection, and repartee, until arriving finally and positively
at the liberty of women, their equality with men—and in this,
its opposition to the Baroque, carried on by men, makes sense.
Placed under the sign of irregularity (and so, of imprecision) which
Barroco designates, and if the imperfections are foremost those of
pearls, its movement quickly approaches the place of desire, of the
instant, of the intuition, and of the urge—whatever the sex-spring
of its spectator, submissions to the work will take place, to ancient
or religious subjects, to its pleasure, these very imperfections. It is
emblematic, this Berninian rape of Proserpina: at every moment the
spectator, by the gazes which the characters and hydra cast on him,
is summoned, his gaze called to, demanded. Named after its creation
(as often happens) by historians whose opposition to the Baroque was
profound (by reason, maybe, of their Protestant faith, with which
notions of rigor, precision, concision, restraint are traditionally
associated), they describe this movement as a response to the Reform
(to contrast it with, perhaps, the French Revolution, according to
the profound changes caused by the two periods). We find here the
opposition, the blade that separates, the judgment, even though the
lips, the forms, in joining, are sutured together (the Reform did
not split a single monotheistic religion into two distinct religions,
but into two subcurrents united by Christianity). Between these
lips, eyelids, one Baroque, the other Precious, in the center, dwell
the eye, the pearl, the clitoris, the soul. If the pearl's imperfection
is the namesake of the Baroque, where the gaze plays such a large
role, the eyes, the site of a powerful enigma, are deemed "mirrors
of the soul" by Preciosity, whereas pearls ornament, threaded along
a string, their necks, like so many dewdrops on arachnid silks—un
labyrinthe de diamante scintillant comme une toile d'araignée—I
can't help but think this necklace should be strung into a sex or an

anus, which threads out, pearl by pearl, looking at it from close-up, the pleasure when, one by one, they get pulled out. Juxtaposed by Bellmer in The Portrait of Unica with the Sex-Eye (1961), at first the eye lodges itself, a preparatory sketch, into the meatus of a cock, to be slid then between the labiae of an anatomically reversed sex, where the clitoris-pearl-eye needs to be fished out from the anus. Story of the Eye. Open, closed, half-closed—split by a blade: split, her lips, the eyelids, can always join back together, cut off this movement, into her water the eye can go, luring with the soul's reflection a withdrawal whose nature, reflective, passionate, will always remain undetermined. The eye is the eye in what holds, holds back, is held, will pierce. The eye is the brooch: Œdipus. His end castrates his sight: desperate, seizing the brooch-eye, pointed, but without being a blade, which gives tissue a form, gives tissue its creases, metonymy of the feminine sex which gives way under its very form, baring the body hung from his wedded mother, unveiling Jocasta's spread legs, Œdipus exposes a pair of scissors. Before the violence of their blades' appearance, and, one supposes, up to date on the practice of epilation in ancient Greece, of the clitoris-eye, perhaps half-closed, labiae-eyelid, this dead eye regarding him even more closely than the repulsed eyes, situated too high, of the dead woman, an initial penetration takes place. Neither enucleation of this organ, nor ablation of what was penetrating, but penetration, in front of what, being round, looks without seeing, of him who looks at what no longer sees in order to see it no longer: an eye for an eye: an eye for a clitoris. Metonymic reproduction in order to reproduce no longer, reproduction in oneself of what happened to the other, penetrating itself with this avowal, the other already dead, dead from having been touched, ending up untouchable to the one who still looked at him then: annihilation of the desire for reproduction by the reproduction of the gesture, the castration of the clitoris-eye by the one who looks then and still sees: insufficiency of the gesture: some pearl-eyes dwell in the meatus-cock-eye which could still, with another clitoris-eye, reproduce something. Equally penetrated, no longer sees, can no longer foresee any reproduction. The impossibility of the brooch-eye is that of slicing; the detachment is not produced; still a lack of gender's absence in the one who has penetrated to the point of going blind, the feminine and masculine. *The feminine nevertheless remains present at its side, will help him and will accompany Antigone, his half-sister-daughter. But no other status, no form aside from this undifferentiated-gendered one will be found before his own death: the masculine returns by grace of Apollo's construction of a consecrated sanctuary. To make the blades of a pair of scissors penetrate, the point of an eye-brooch, to lodge them in flesh, the heart or the eye, requires strength and violence, an impotence which, given that they may still move around in the resulting wound or get stuck in the mass of torn tissue, unsublimable, only causing pain to exist there. And yet if the matter is fine enough, soft,* bɯɒor *flexible—in short, alive—the scissors allow one, after the initial gash, the scissors now removed, and open, to slide one of the blades into the wound's interior, leaving the other one on the exterior and thus to open them, like phallic blades, from the center to the exterior... It is like this that Madeleine de Scudery's gesture should be seen, who, after having, with necessary violence, in response to the historical context, driven her scissors, Preciosity, into the masculine mass, an eye or the heart, carves out her part of the sublime, without however completely opening up a place for the feminine, the spawning of her sexuality—at least so her Sapphic practice can be efficient. Their first use is solar, Dionysian, the blades part from one another, around the clitoris-axis, open, not without danger (so, pleasure is mingling with danger?), the legs sharp, the vulva is accessible, as the spreading of lips they are soon to create in the masculine, proposing to them this thing it holds, not only assuring the existence of the feminine in the feminine, by way of cutting precision, the singular and masculine kind found in a chisel, but also to find out what femininity exists in this male-self, what lips can be opened there. Of this eternal return, the feminine only has to make, the plural scissors embrace the feminine and masculine, and inherently past, present, and future—much like Atropos, who, in the darkness, decides Man's fate. Thus, short of a violent impediment that a women may live out, reassuring oneself with cutting precision remains a masculine affair, tending to attain the feminine, attempting to find it. Once the search leads to the figure of the mother, to find again the known form of a feminine, such an Œdipus, castration occurs: if another essence is discovered in it, then the acted-on chisels realize a sublimation—and search in a matter that grows harder and harder, thus more durable: precise, sinks into the flesh, Persephone's thigh, into the marble, the hand, which the acted-on chisels sculpt. From the half-open, provoked, & efficient, doubly desired, comes a bivalent pleasure. Reflective and passionate vulva. Sex and soul; soul and sex. Relying like this, despite all its desire for e(rectilely e)levated feeling, on sex, however much she opposed it, the position held by Scudery is Cornellian. While, in the narrow margins left by social context, the Nobles of the Gown, it may have been precious, its engagement was precise. Sublimation of the respect, the correctness, carried by the person and her language, of the etiquette learned since childhood—Madeleine de Scudery was approached to be the nanny of Mazarin's nieces. From the Baroque to Preciosity to the French Revolution, from Romanticism and the rise of a new social class in the 19th century, the bourgeoisie wanted to imitate the nobility. Then appeared the handbooks of good manners, grammars of politesse, that no faux-pas might spoil the pleasure (of a soiree, of a salon) that comes from codes being applied to the letter, that "everything harmonize in perfect pitch," this precision of music, in correctness, thus, the very greatest correction concerning guests as hosts. Paradigmatically, the literary movement of Preciosity finds its sexual twin in fetishism. Precision and correctness, inherent in good manners, are indispensable to it. The peak of pleasure (which, here, is not necessarily orgasm) is rooted in the ritual, the scenario, is achieved in the slightest details. The present is anticipated entirely so as to be realized as perfectly as possible. Improvisation, before it appears, is rooted out, cut off, castrated. Fetishism, a transfer operated onto an inanimate object, translates, into psychoanalysis, the anxiety of castration, rendered actually possible by the use of tools created for their precision. It is through precision that the Baroque, by other codes and other techniques, is likewise able to attain, like the Preciosity-Fetishism couple, its sexual corollary, BDSM. It has already been underscored, the importance of the gaze, which attunes the Baroque's to that of the voyeur, submitting it to an expressed urge, eventually religious, as in the Ecstasy of Saint Theresa by the selfsame Cavaliere. "I saw in his hand a long golden lance, at whose tip one almost believed burned a small fire." The Baroque carries this relationship to its peak. Bernini's chisel allows for the creation of an object both submissive and subduing, resembling to a T the relationship of a dominant-dominated couple. If the anxiety of castration is sublimated, by means of its projection onto an object, according to the Precious fetishists, this same anxiety, in BDSM, in the Baroque, is not displaced during its sublimation, but played out, directly, presently, staged, in a new way every time, inspired by History, be it ancient, religious, artistic. No surprise to see in the practice of bondage, at which excel those whose culture is precise down to its cuisine, the Japanese, the resumption of a theme dear to the Baroque, almost a trademark, the contrapposto, this squirming, twisting of the body, coursing with urges, forces, desires, even contradictory ones. As in fetishism, a ritual is established but it is based on the contract, deemed Sadomasochistic, which master and slave commit to respect. In all ways, master and mistress are responsible for the slave's good health; and, more than a right, it is a duty to the one who is being dominated, to whom explicitly submit the dominators. Thus the BDSM-Baroque precision is that of the ever-present, that of intertwined relationships, as intellectual as they are physical, between the subjects. Where fetishism forbids improvisation, BDSM allows, in a sense, the opposite, to go always further, to invent more and more strongly, until the very death—just as J.L. Borges, in his Universal History of Infamy (1954) prophecies: "I would call Baroque the style that deliberately exhausts (or attempts to exhaust) all of its possibilities, and which brushes against its own caricature, [...] the final step of all art once it exposes and dissipates its medium." Thus the Baroque topples into the Rococo, suffocation, the topographical view, war-like, of the smallest part, even interior, of the smallest surface now covered over, decorated, scarified, tattooed. From the Baroque to Preciosity to the French Revolution, Philippe Sollers notes that "the discomfort over these questions is more and more palpable: how does it happen that we passed in a mere few years from Sade's Juliette to Madame Bovary? Or rather, how does it happen that suddenly, with Romanticism taking hold of this affair, everything blurs to the point that one derives very singular experiences from it?" But then, why a handbook of good sexual practices? How to constitute it, make it clear, precise, detailed, and for what discounted result? What blade would it be? The sexual revolution saw this type of work flourish. Discovered through the parental library's intervention. Which contained, by Robert Chartam, Male Sexuality and Female Sexuality, published in 1971. Beyond the possible neurotic consequences that a psychoanalysis would have to elucidate (the consciousness of reading books my parents had bought with the objective of, upon their completion, having better sex), no doubt this had, pragmatically speaking, consequences on my sexual practices (through this consciousness of reading a work addressed to men and its companion volume addressed to women, by the hand of the same author: I could, in a way, become a man and a woman). Written in a language now remembered as simple, detailed, descriptive, precise, contrary to older or more poetic works (erotic poetics can only contain the simplest language, the distancing of its risk is the experience of a double disappointment, disappointment in literature being added to disappointment in the sensual), steeping myself without repulsion or taboo, but with pleasure, in ideas of*

138

fellatio, sodomy, having however no sexual practice. We often hear said, today, of films (pornos among others—although my teenage memories, of great sexual pleasure, which derive from films, are not associated with this genre), that they have an influence on the practice of the generation which can, with easy access and without having to wait very long (no Sunday night scrambled screen viewings, keeping an eye out while waiting for the right circumstances to watch alone; and then: TV shows whose setting is a brothel, some pornographic enterprise, etc.), on the internet, to access there, without the referents, the limits, the edges that come together there, opened by this intermediary. This subtle conjunction of the social body's attempt at homogenization (politics as written, oral, cinematographic, sonic traditions—Trick Me!) in the singularity of each body will not exactly bring about, in each, the same reactions (on that note, the precision that the कामसूत्र *, or the Kāma Sūtra, ancestor of all sexual handbooks?, bears on the woman (deer, mare, elephant) and man (hare, bull, horse) for quantifying the depth and size of their genitals is not uninteresting). Philippe Sollers, again, says, "[to] believe in effect that, in response to those questions, only experience should speak. To know—in the first person singular as much as possible what's at play once a body, with its language, mingles with this kind of question." In sum, and very relative to my own experience, a sexual handbook, whose scope of knowledge occurs upstream from a sexuality, like those good manners, the etiquette taught to children, seems possibly useful if it is not infantilizing and if it is sufficiently transgressive—may the search it inspires not be Œdipian . . . Every practice becomes possible because the idea of a solar pleasure becomes associated with it then, named. What's more, disarray for those men and women deprived of intuition (Baroque) and learning (Preciosity) who want to become, through the precision conferred by either approach, good students: neither handbook nor accepted method, always practicing to make perfect: finger on the clitoris, hand gripping the cock, mouth kissing the other* *mouth, the other sex: it's always the same and it should always be different—when a man fingers me, the worry over precision and imprecision are conjoined. Geographic precision: yes, my clitoris is there, you found it, bravo, you found that little eminence, there, yes, it's there, happy you noticed, been a while that I've known, myself: it becomes unbearable, the pleasure is too sharp, not even echolalia, it's identical, sliced, the goal that isn't the goal has been accomplished. So it be enough, and I move around finger(s), hand, to adjust, so the pleasure not be vague, but so it invade, not lingering at the edges of sensation. But to make this gesture often means the mechanization of the gesture, the third possibility of precision, unbearable, pleasure shattered by the handbook of good sexual manners, as soon as it is read, known, learned, applied to the letter. More unbearable still when I can feel someone else's requirements in the gestures used. My ideal of precision lies in the search, the discovery of a motif, precious because non-topological, which I do not know because it is reproduced and modified, to the rhythm of my changing face, my eyes half-closed, mouth partially open, the interlacings misplaced, accelerated, held back, a shifting Baroque refrain, irregular and yet precise, cutting me like scissors, plural and singular, feminine and masculine, listening to my moaning, sighs, cries, improvising to the extent it has been discovered, multiple orgasms, knowing to stop when at the limits of another world, an August evening, I seem to be tumbling. Precision is this precious present.*

The written doesn't remain.
  The spoken is remains.
      The spoken produces an indelible debt.
        ~~Debt fertilizes acts through~~ its
transfers. We take recourse to the imaginary to
    get an idea of the real, write it out   *more or less 50*
    get in to give you an idea of what the imaginary means
                      covering with forgetting and
                      romanticism   i f
                      given so much time, time
                      time, time of
transfer

      Love needs reality.
That's why beauty and reality are identical.
          Because beauty means a possible end to
fright.

cultural
gradients
°uᵗ ᵒʳ ˢⁱᵈᵉ
grossesse
&
become animal
&
become mechanism

cultural
gradients
°uᵗ ᵒʳ ˢⁱᵈᵉ
grossesse
&
become animal
&
become mechanism

gradients
culturels
°uᵗ ᵒʳ ˢⁱᵈᵉ
grossesse
&
become animal
&
become mechanism

* *

Here, I base my movements on the movements of my heart.

Every day, I have to contend with the patriarchal model; this is neither joyous nor simple. And wouldn't it be harder, if I believe the movements of my heart, to have to contend with a society (which has never existed, reproduction of precedent, a mirror inventing the relationship of forces) that were matriarchal—arkein from power, authority, bending over, enduring it down below while placing it on high, dominators dominated and dominated dominators get along; their machine, like every machine, is functional. I don't want to submit myself anymore, and, in submitting myself, still suffer, and suffering from submitting and making suffer, if the occasion, age, or position, gives me the chance to, mechanism of the unstoppable flux. The oppressor makes of the oppressed, who finds some diminished reflection of his oppressor's place, the fervent upholder of his order. This is not theoretical, I've seen it in the eyes of women, having suffered, suffering, making suffer, aged, taking revenge on their (step-)*daughters.*

* *

The movements of my heart tell me no, don't put your finger in the gears of this machine, and if the machine brutalizes the finger, understand it, but don't take part in it, don't deny it, describe it, but don't take part in it,

elles et eux ont pourtant chassé ensemble
quelques-un,es pourtant ont inventé ensemble
sexuel,les et anthropomorphique,s
god,déesse,es

144

mais ni toutes et tous ni ensemble
mais les autres qui
resistant,   defiant   to   the   back-to-back
masculine and feminine, human and animal,
animate and inanimate,   and   ,
mais qui défiait, *ces* autres *qui, resistant to the*
value-granting gradations, what children did
they have? It's possible to revere the difference,
hommage paid to a set of many who believe in
the inside itself of an in-between the state of
differences, without an original hierarchy, this
origin given as extant, if the origin is still necessary.
Oof. Breathe. It's possible. The movements of my
heart are certain of it, my reason in doubt, what
children did they have?
* *

The movements of my heart are invisible, my heart is
in my body; my heart is in a society's body; infused
by vision: and overrules seeing, seer, visible, visible
lends power. Gestation (human) *is visible. Power*
provokes jealousy. Jealousy is gestative of oppodivision
when fed with ignorance of equal implication,
masculine and feminine, human and animal,
animate and inanimate,   and   ,
in life, *what children did they have?*
* *

The movements of my heart tell me that all genders
& all ages are necessary and vivacious Umwelt,en so
that, together,—what? something about joy, yes? Yes?
Breathe. The movements of my heart tell me breathe,
surrender, surrender the only reason, and ^{don't panic}
* *

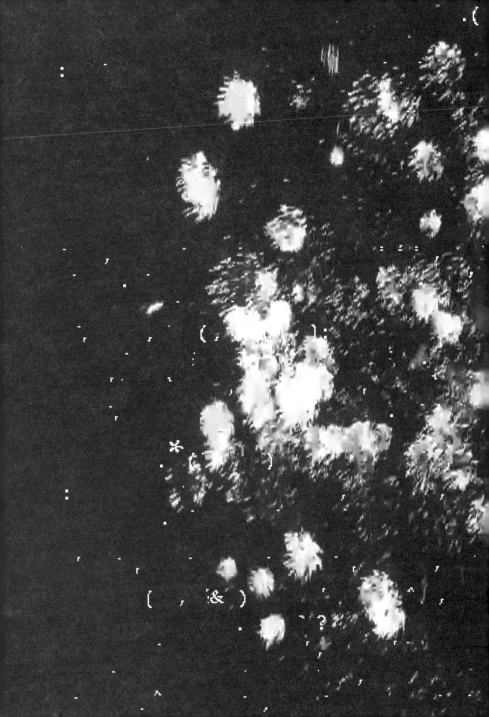

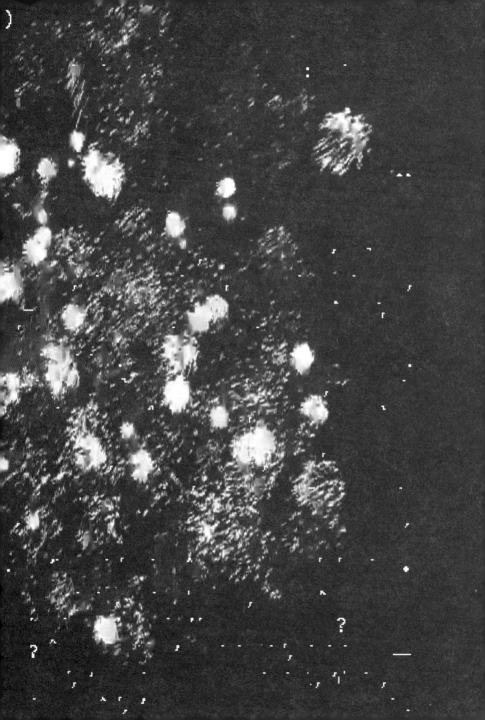

ABOUT THE AUTHOR

Anne Kawala was born in 1980 in Herlincourt, a small town in northern France. She's been awarded grants and residencies by the French National Book Centre, Moly Sabata, the Akademie Schloss Solitude, the Chartreuse in Villeneuve lez Avignon, and elsewhere. Her books include *F.aire L.a F.eui||e (f.l.f)* (Le clou dans le fer, 2008), *Le cowboy et le poète (Chevauchépris)* (L'attente, 2011), *part &* (Joca Seria, 2011), *De la rose et du renard, leurs couleurs et odeurs,* (CipM, IFs Beyrouth / Saïda, 2012), *Le déficit indispensable (screwball)* (Sarl Al Dante, 2016), and *Au cœur du cœur de l'écrin* (Editions Lanskine). She lives in Nantes.

In writing this book, the author benefited from assistance from the Centre National du Livre, from the "Des écrivains en impesanteur" program of the Centre National des Études Spatiales, and from a residence at Akademie Schloss Solitude, which also provided a grant to fund the book's translation into English.

ABOUT THE TRANSLATOR

Kit Schluter was born in 1989 in Boston, Massachusetts. Among his published and forthcoming translations are books by Amandine André, Anne Kawala, Clamenç Llansana, Jaime Saenz, Michel Surya, Julio Torri, and numerous collections by Marcel Schwob. He is recipient of a National Endowment for the Arts translation fellowship, as well as "Discovery"/*Boston Review* and Glascock prizes, and holds an mfa in poetry from Brown University. Kit co-edits O'clock Press, and lives in Mexico City. More at www.kitschluter.com

He would like to thank Joshua Edwards, Forrest Gander, Elaine Kahn, Robert Kelly, Trisha Low, Charlotte Mandell, Nathanaël, Cole Swensen, Keith Waldrop, Rosmarie Waldrop, Lynn Xu, and Jeffrey Zuckerman for their company and guidance in writing throughout the translation of this book. With special thanks to Anne Kawala, for her contributions to, and oversight of, this translation.